disc

you will be ruined,

the viscount said.

"I'm prepared to face the consequences."

"One thing more, so there will be no further misunderstanding. I sent my lawyer to Cambridge yesterday to learn what he could about your circumstances. It seems you told me the truth."

"Of course!" exclaimed Caroline indignantly.

"You forget, my dear Miss Pennington, I have reason to know you're not always scrupulously honest. And, at the risk of sounding immodest, I am considered a matrimonial prize. A number of young ladies have gone to very peculiar lengths to entice me to the altar."

"How fortunate for them they failed," Caroline snapped, her impetuous tongue betraying her once again.

"You're a sharp-tongued baggage, aren't you?"

He watched her intently for a moment longer before walking over to face her. He extended his hand, and Caroline took it timidly. Pulling her to her feet, he held her hand captive, his thumb rubbing her palm. And Caroline felt her breath quicken . . .

THE SCANDALOUS MISS

THE SCANDALOUS MISS

Donna Bell

PAGEANT BOOKS

Publisher's Note: This is a work of fiction. The characters, incidents, and dialogues are products of the author's imagination and are not to be construed as real. Any resemblance to actual events or persons, living or dead, is entirely coincidental.

PAGEANT BOOKS
225 Park Avenue South
New York, New York 10003

Copyright © 1988 by Donna Bell

All rights reserved. The right to reproduce this book or portions thereof in any form must be obtained in writing from the Permissions Department of the publisher.

PAGEANT and colophon are trademarks of the publisher

Cover artwork by Franco Accornero

Printed in the U.S.A.

First Pageant Books printing: December, 1988

10 9 8 7 6 5 4 3 2 1

In memory of my mother, whose greatest legacy to her children is her love of books

THE SCANDALOUS MISS

pass," murmured his friend as he continued to stare at the shelves.

"That's right, Robert." The little man wondered at his friend's abstracted manner. "I say, you're not feeling bad about telling old Christopher you don't want the filly, are you? Horses are business, you know."

Viscount Rosemeade turned a puzzled gaze on his friend. "What are you running on about now, Ferdie?"

"What? Oh, nothing." Ferdie lapsed into silence.

The door was pushed open, and a rather scruffy-looking footman appeared bearing a silver tray that contained two glasses and a decanter. The servant's unusual appearance was due more to his face than to anything else. A long saber scar curled downward from the bottom of one ear, following the line of his jaw. His gray brows, unlike his heavily pomaded hair, were scraggly, giving the middle-aged servant a continual look of inquiry. He walked with a slight limp. But his livery was neat and he wore it with flair.

"Just put it on the table, Boggs."

"Very good, Major—I mean, m'lord," said the footman.

Farningham rolled his eyes at his friend. Rosemeade ignored him.

The servant poured the ruby liquid and then presented each gentleman with a glass.

"How's the leg, Boggs?" asked the viscount.

"Tolerable, m'lord, thank ye."

"Good. And how are you getting on here?"

"Very well, m'lord. I thank the stars every day for ye and Captain Wyndridge getting me my place here."

Rosemeade smiled. " 'Twas the least we could do after you saved my brother from that scavenger's knife."

Boggs shifted uncomfortably. "May I ask, Lord Rosemeade, if ye've had word of Captain Wyndridge?"

"No, nothing in the last month. But, as we both know, his orders are often of an unusual nature. I daresay I'll have a response from him soon."

The servant bowed his way out.

Ferdie Farningham ran his stubby fingers through his mousy-brown hair. After closing the book, he sat down in a soft chair, his feet barely touching the floor.

"You know, Robert, your getting the club to take on Boggs is an excellent indicator of the power you wield here at White's. He's the least servile servant I've ever met. Always appearing out of the blue, always studying a body from under those great, bushy eyebrows of his. It's a bit unnerving."

"Not when you've served with him in a Peninsula campaign. Best batman a soldier could ask for. Knowing he was to be under Garrett's command was the only reason I purchased colors for my brother."

Ferdie considered this a moment, then asked,

"Robert, what has the Home Office told you about Garrett's disappearance?"

"Nothing. That's why I know he was sent on a secret mission, possibly across enemy lines. But not a word to anyone, mind you, Ferdie. There are unfriendly ears, even in the heart of London."

Farningham's eyes slid around the room as if he were about to discover someone hiding in the stacks, and Viscount Rosemeade returned to his scrutiny of the shelves.

"You know, Ferdie, this so-called library is a disgrace. I realize most of our members come to White's to gamble or to escape domestic bliss, but this room is part of the club, after all. It shouldn't look as though someone just threw the books on the shelves."

Ferdie shook his head wonderingly at this new maggot that had gotten into his friend's head and returned to his perusal of bloodlines and racing stock, trying to trace the lines of a colt he'd seen at Tattersall's.

Viscount Rosemeade sat down among the chaos and began to read titles on the row of shelves beside him.

"This is ridiculous! Look here, Ferdie!" he commanded.

Ferdie Farningham obliged his friend by drawing closer and pretending to be interested.

"Just look at this! No order—no sense. Here's Locke's *Treatise on Government* with *Tristram Shandy* on one side, Bunyan's *Pilgrim's Progress* and the works of Aristotle on the other! Chaos, total chaos!" Rosemeade muttered darkly.

Ferdie didn't really see anything wrong with the titles mentioned (not that he'd had occasion to read any of them—except for a few choice passages from *Tristram Shandy*, of course), but he clucked obligingly.

"Well, Robert, what can be done about it? I mean, every time some old blackguard up and dies, he leaves his 'collection' to his club. Or someone—for some reason—buys a book. After he's read it, what's he to do with it? I mean, it's no good to him, right? So he gives it to his club."

Ferdie was enjoying himself immensely, envisioning other stories that would account for the great number of books, but Rosemeade interrupted by thumping his friend's knee heartily.

"That's it! I had a don at Cambridge. What was his name? Taught me Latin, or tried to. Penn? Penenger? Pennington! That was it! A real right one, as we would have said. Up to every rig and row before we could pull it! But I remember he loved books. I went to his home once and he showed me his library. It was so neat, so organized. He explained to me how he had catalogued every volume. It was fascinating!"

"Good God, Robert! Never say you mean to do that here!"

"Not I! Professor Pennington. I shall write to him immediately. He could come to London to do this job. Something to occupy his long holiday this summer."

"I think you've got to be queer in your attic to

want to bother at all, Robert, but if you say so. . . ."

"Well, I do, Ferdie, I most assuredly do!"

"I cannot countenance this mad scheme, Caroline!" exclaimed Olivia Stanton, shuddering delicately.

"Nevertheless, I intend to go through with it, Livie. It is either this or the house must be sold." Turning to see herself better in the looking glass, Caroline Pennington did not appear in the least unnerved by her unorthodox image.

True, she admitted, her tall, willowy frame looked youthful rather than manly or feminine, with her bosom bound tightly and a man's frock coat settled on her narrow shoulders. But the dark brown curls framing her face softened the square chin and well-defined cheekbones. The candid brown eyes were round and pleasing. She smiled at her reflection. The expression brought a vitality to her face, revealing something of her inquisitive, often impulsive nature.

Miss Stanton's disapproving face appeared beside her image. Caroline's tall figure dressed in men's garments provided a striking contrast to her companion's. Miss Stanton was just over five feet in height, and though her figure was trim, it boasted ample valleys and curves. Her lavender morning gown was trimmed with lace and ribbons, and her fair-complexioned face was topped by sandy-blond ringlets that bobbed as she shook her head.

"But, Caroline, think! To go to London—by yourself, practically—and dressed like that!"

"I think the breeches fit quite nicely," she murmured innocently.

"Indeed they do, and that is just the point! I hope I am too old to be considered missish, but you simply cannot masquerade in such a costume. It is shocking!"

"Nonsense! I realize it is not at all the thing, but it is necessary. And no one need ever know, Livie," she pleaded.

"But what if someone guesses? How many students do you think we should have if it became known that the headmistress paraded around London for two months in men's breeches?"

"At least I am wearing them and not 'in' them, as you say," Caroline said outrageously, hoping to lighten the mood.

"Caroline Pennington!"

"Very well, Livie. I'll cry peace, if you will. But know this: With or without your blessing, I must carry out this scheme. Until I received the viscount's letter, I thought we would truly be reduced to begging in the streets. And now! With the commission he offers, I'll be able to set up our little school in style. What's more, I shan't be forced to sell Papa's house. I don't know if I could bear to part with it. It's all I have left."

Wisely, Caroline forebore to add how excited she was about the proposed journey. The scheme had been born of desperation, but the mad plan had given Caroline's life a focus again. Mourning her father had been more than a matter of putting on a black gown. She had felt lost, an unaccustomed problem for the decisive young woman of three and twenty.

So she plunged into this masquerade eagerly, her impulsive nature satisfied by its audacity, while her sensible side grasped this practical solution to her monetary dilemma.

Her companion, though a mere thirty-five years old, drew herself up like the most terrifying matron at Almack's. Fixing her former charge with a stifling stare, she intoned, "You do have me, Caroline."

"Yes, Livie, I could not forget you," said Caroline simply, turning and giving her a quick hug. "After all, you have been with me since I turned eight. Do you ever recall that first meeting?"

"Every time I forget myself and try to bully you into doing things my way. You were positively horrid that first day."

"Wasn't I? Telling Papa I would *not* have some awful woman trying to take my mother's place, or call you aunt, even if we were distantly related."

Olivia touched Caroline's dark curls fondly. "I found you tottering along the top of the garden wall. You wouldn't even look at me, so I hitched up my skirts and joined you."

Caroline turned to Olivia. "Can you join me in this, too, Livie? Can you try to understand?"

Thus, they began their plans for a rather unusual debut.

"You'll need Hessians, a hat, gloves . . . Oh,

just everything. We'll tell the Bateses about our plans; Mr. Bates can make the purchases for us. And cravats. You shall certainly need several. I shall endeavor to teach you a simple, though acceptable, method of tying one," said Olivia, adding to her list as she spoke.

"And how would you know about tying a cravat?" inquired Caroline with great curiosity.

The other woman blushed becomingly and muttered, "Never you mind, miss. Just never you mind."

Two weeks later, Caroline Pennington sat perched on the edge of the seat of a hackney cab exclaiming at each novel sight that struck her eyes.

Her collar points were not fashionably high, for this would not have done for a man of letters. Her cravat was simple, something Livie called a waterfall. The brown serge jacket and buff-colored waistcoat fitted her loosely; the breeches were cut to mask her shapely legs. She wore riding boots, although they had traveled by stage and not by horseback.

Her brunette curls had been sacrificed to "the cause," and the result was a neat, though outmoded, queue tied with a narrow ribbon of brown grosgrain. The curls had disguised her well-defined cheekbones and longish straight nose; they had shrouded the strong square chin.

When Caroline had turned to see her image that first time, dressed as she was now, her ego had suffered a sharp twist, for staring back at her

The Scandalous Miss

was a handsome young gentleman, not the pretty young woman she had been. She had moved closer to the mirror to inspect her face, trying to determine how an attractive female (for she had been told she was) could change so drastically.

It had taken every waking second of the two-week interval before Olivia had pronounced her ready. She had had to learn to walk instead of gliding gracefully. Her mannerisms, her way of sitting, her preferences in beverages were decidedly feminine. Finally, however, she could tromp across the room, flop into a chair, and sip from the large brandy snifter without betraying the least hesitation. The last proved to be only a limited success; the smallest quantity of liquor went straight to her head, leaving her weak and dizzy.

Olivia smiled indulgently at her charge, then turned back to the view on her side of the carriage. Her fine gray eyes missed no detail of the scene. Indeed, she seemed almost as young as her friend, her own excitement adding a youthful vitality to her countenance.

"And a bright good mornin' to ye, lovely lady," called a street vendor as the traffic caused the hackney driver to pull up. "I've some lovely fruit here for a lovely lady."

Olivia blushed in confusion and stammered, "No, I don't think . . ."

"Ach! Ye misunderstand, me lady, 'tis a gift to a fair flower." With this, the vendor bowed low, his eyes twinkling, and passed two perfect peaches through the carriage window and into Olivia Stanton's lap. She gasped and began to protest when suddenly their hackney lumbered on. Caroline contained her laughter long enough to shout a thank-you to the audacious street vendor.

"Quite a feat, my dear! In London only half an hour and you've already made a conquest!"

"Caroline, stop that! I've done no such thing!"

"That's what happens when a young female pokes her head out the carriage window. Most unbecoming!"

"You were doing the same thing, Caroline Pennington," countered Olivia.

"Ah, but I am a young man. It makes all the difference."

"Young man, indeed," Olivia mouthed. "Have you thought what you shall say if your cousin, Mr. Wickersham, decides to return to London early?"

"Cousin Penn is in Scotland shooting grouse or some such thing. I don't see why he should suddenly return to London. He hates the Season. And I did ask if we might use his house for the summer. If he planned to return, he would have refused. You'll feel much more comfortable when the Bateses arrive and Penn's servants have gone on holiday."

"Perhaps, but—"

"Now, Livie," Caroline began coaxingly, "no more fretting. We are in London. Think of all the sights we shall see!"

"Sights we've seen before with the professor," said Miss Stanton sensibly.

"Some of them, of course. But you and I will

have so much more freedom this time. As my 'widowed aunt,' you may go when and where you please. And I, of course, can go anywhere."

"Yes! Any place of ill repute you care to name!"

"But I can't name a single one!" Caroline laughed.

"Yet, you mean to, young lady. I only hope your impetuous nature doesn't lead you into some situation, some danger—"

"Oh, Livie!" Caroline smiled becomingly at her companion. "I promise to behave like the quiet, dull, studious young man I appear to be. After all, the viscount would scarcely approve me if I act like a callow youth."

"Hmm. But, Caroline, that's another thing. You really should have written to Lord Rosemeade and explained that the professor is dead and that, as his 'son,' you felt qualified to replace him. The viscount shall very likely decide against the younger Mr. Charles Pennington, my dear."

"Well, I would think it very shabby of him to disqualify me just because of my youth."

Olivia Stanton's laughter rang clearly in the morning air. "If your eyes flash at him like that and you throw your chest out in that manner, the viscount will develop quite different ideas about you, 'Mr.' Pennington!"

Caroline grinned an impish little grin that looked anything but masculine; then she lounged against the squabs of the cab, her pose a veritable study of masculine leisure.

"We're here, Caroline," said Olivia Stanton gently.

"What? Ah, yes, let me help you down, Aunt," said young Mr. Pennington solicitously.

Ascending the steps to Cousin Penn's redbrick town house, it would have been impossible to say who dreaded to cross the threshold more. One second, Caroline was leading the way; the next, Olivia was almost dragging her forward. Olivia grabbed the knocker and sounded it briskly. The door was opened by a footman in dull blue livery.

"Yes?" asked the formidable butler.

"I am Charles Pennington. And this is my aunt, Mrs. Stanton. You must be Biggers."

"Yes, sir. Won't you come in? Mr. Wickersham told us to expect you."

As they followed him into the hallway, Caroline squeezed Olivia's trembling hand, which rested on her arm.

"You'll wish to refresh yourselves," intoned the butler.

"A bath would be delightful, Biggers," replied Miss Stanton, surprised by her own firm tone.

"Yes, madam. I shall give the orders."

"And for myself as well, Biggers," said Caroline with a calm she wished she felt.

"Very good, sir. I shall also send refreshments. Mr. Wickersham dined at eight, but of course. . . ."

"Eight is perfect."

During this time they had been climbing the staircase and had now arrived at Miss Stanton's room. "Since your abigail hasn't yet arrived, I shall send Milly to you, if that is convenient."

"Very good, Biggers," replied Olivia, thinking the girl could unpack her trunk at least.

Caroline continued down the hall with Biggers until they entered an airy room that was dominated by massive dark furniture. The numerous windows filled the room with sunlight, a stark contrast to the mahogany wood. She had obviously been placed in her cousin's own room.

"I see you did not bring your valet, sir. I shall be happy to assist you with your bath until other arrangements have been made."

Caroline stifled a gasp. Recovering quickly, she said, "That's not at all necessary, Biggers, I assure you. I am accustomed to dressing and bathing myself."

"Very well, sir," said Biggers. "If you should require anything, there is a bellpull by the bed and another by the dressing table."

"Two?"

"Yes, sir. Mr. Wickersham doesn't wish to rise in order to ring whether he is abed or dressing."

Caroline hid her amazement, only murmuring, "I see. That will be all, Biggers."

As the last covers were removed, Olivia rose and left Caroline to her port. Caroline slowly sipped the potent liquid, willing her limbs to remain still and relaxed. She threw one elegant leg over the arm of the chair, lounging negligently. Biggers quietly directed the footman to clear the table, seemingly unaware of her existence. Caroline, however, was acutely conscious of the butler's every move, every glance. She realized that if she could not deceive Biggers, her first true audience, she would be forced to abandon her desperate scheme.

"Do you require anything else, sir?"

"Thank you, no. Ah, Biggers, there is one thing. I must compose a note; I assume there is paper in the salon."

"In the secretary, sir. I shall set out the materials myself."

"Never mind, Biggers. I can find them." With this, Caroline rose and stretched languidly. She sauntered down the hall and into the salon, closing the door casually.

Olivia looked up from her embroidery expectantly. Caroline sank wearily into the closest chair, expelling a loud *whoosh* of breath.

"So?" asked Olivia impatiently.

Caroline looked up suddenly, the trace of a grin growing wider.

"I'll do. I'll do."

"What is it, Ferdie? I've an urgent matter I need to attend to immediately!" barked Lord Rosemeade.

"Urgent?" queried his companion. "My dear Robert, nothing is more *urgent* than Holier Than Thou!"

The viscount paused in midstride and eyed his old friend with an amused grin that lightened his rather stern features.

"Very well, Mr. Farningham. What news is it you're bursting to relate?"

"Mallory wants to sell his stud. Foolish, I think, but he always was. You can get him if you act quickly. No one else knows yet."

Rosemeade's brow furrowed briefly. "Then buy him. You will see to it for me, won't you?" An unnecessary question, he knew.

"Certainly! And I wager I get him at a much better price than you could, Robert!"

"I'd not waste the ready on such a wager, Ferdie. I'm not so foolish as Mallory."

"My lord," interrupted the viscount's old butler. "Mr. Pennington is in the library."

"Thank you, Lane." The viscount turned back to Ferdie. "Let me know if you add the stud to my stable, Ferdie. And don't get so carried away that you take him down to Rosemeade and start breeding him without telling me. I should like some say in the matter."

Ferdie Farningham failed to note the amused gleam in the viscount's eyes. Animal husbandry was no topic for joking; he drew himself up to his full height—a mere five and a half feet.

"If you believe I would serve you such an underhanded trick, I'm surprised you trust me to—"

But Rosemeade threw back his head and laughed.

Ferdie blinked twice and shook his head resignedly. Robert could be positively bizarre at times.

At the viscount's shout of laughter, Caroline

leaped away from the fireplace in fright, thus losing her calm, studious pose. She reached up to pat her hair into place, then whipped her hand behind her back, realizing the act was blatantly feminine.

The door opened. Caroline stole a quick glance at the mirror over the mantel; the reflected man was pleasing—for a female.

Lord Rosemeade paused on the threshold, observing his guest with surprise. His gaze flitted around the room and returned to rest on the slender young man.

"Mr. Pennington?"

"Yes, my lord," squeaked Caroline. She cleared her throat and continued in her own throaty voice. "I'm Charles Pennington; I was given my father's name."

"I'm sorry, Mr. Pennington. When I received your father's letter, I expected . . . Or was it your letter?"

"Mine, I'm afraid. I realize you are confused. My father died nine months ago, my lord. I'm only carrying on as he would have wished."

She paused, holding her breath. The viscount's expression remained puzzled as he mentally reviewed past communications with this young Mr. Pennington. He crossed the room and seated himself behind the huge mahogany desk. Caroline shifted uncomfortably, looking exactly like a nervous student caught on some lark.

Rosemeade rested his elbows on the arms of his chair, placed his fingertips together, and peered through the little "steeple" unmercifully.

Chapter One

"It's here someplace, Robert. I saw it only yesterday."

"The book is not essential, Ferdie," drawled the tall man in the overstuffed easy chair, his gray eyes reflecting his unconcern. "There is no need to trouble yourself further."

"It is important, dammit," his friend replied. "I can't bear to lose something when I know it's there. It's a matter of principle that I find the thing!" Ferdie Farningham growled as he tossed several books off a table. He stood on tiptoe, straining to see the titles of the volumes that lined the upper shelves, his small form barely reaching the fifth shelf.

"There it is!" Ferdie shouted suddenly, causing his friend to raise his brows in polite inquiry. "Up there, top row: *Introduction to a General Stud*

Book." The stocky little man slipped as he tried to gain footing on the second shelf. "Agh! Blast that . . . !"

"Now, now, Ferdie, where is it?"

The smaller man pointed to his quarry grudgingly. His friend unfolded his long legs and stood languidly.

Robert Wyndridge, Viscount Rosemeade, had a pleasing face; it was one of classical lines though the nose was a trifle narrow. His chestnut hair was worn in the new windswept, but on Lord Rosemeade's tanned visage the style appeared natural rather than contrived. He was tall and lean, his muscular frame denoting a penchant for sports.

He had long been the object of hopeful mothers' matrimonial pursuit, but at the age of three and thirty, he remained unencumbered. The viscount was certainly of an age to think of setting up his nursery, but having neither mother nor sisters to press him, he preferred to "put it off" as long as possible.

He plucked the elusive tome from the ramshackle shelves and placed it in his companion's hands. Ferdie wasted no time in perusing the volume for the proof he sought to back his arguments.

"There! You see, Robert," he began triumphantly. "Silver Lady, by Silverlining, out of Silver Dawn, and both were sired by Break O'Day."

"Quite so. Yes, you were right, Ferdie. Too much inbreeding. I think I shall let the mare

Beads of perspiration popped out on Caroline's brow. She longed to run her finger along the inside of her collar but felt paralyzed by the harsh gray eyes that held hers. Suddenly, the viscount's brows rose and his lips curved in a secret smile. Now he recalled it: yes, he had once met Professor Pennington's young offspring—a charming child and decidedly feminine.

The viscount straightened. "Why?"

"I, uh, I beg your pardon?"

"Why did you perpetrate such a deception, young man? For surely you won't deny that you set out to deceive me?"

"No, my lord," admitted Caroline. She quickly decided that the truth—or part of it, at least—was all that would satisfy the tall, taciturn gentleman before her.

"It's true, I did set out to deceive you. My reason was twofold. I will lose my father's house without this commission. And, my lord, if I had written you the truth, you would most certainly have refused to give such a commission to someone of my youth."

When the viscount nodded, she added, "You would not even have taken into account that I have worked closely with my father for years and am quite as capable as he of executing this commission."

Her breathing was shallow as she finished. Calm, she thought, calm. The silence dragged on.

"But did it not occur to you, my dear young man, that I would never consider employing a person who could be dishonest with me?" the viscount asked.

He was surprised to see his nervous visitor stiffen, the muscles in the jaw tighten. Caroline bowed. Her throat had constricted, and she felt close to tears. He couldn't turn her down now, but he surely would if she cried. What matter now if I do give way to my tears like the female I am? she thought. But she forced herself to look steadily at the cold man behind the desk. Her pride lent her composure.

"Then I'll bid you good day, my lord," she said with quiet dignity.

Caroline's hand was on the doorknob when the viscount called out, "Wait, Mr. Pennington."

She halted but did not turn around.

"Can you catalogue the books?"

She looked over her shoulder. "I can."

"Just as your father would have?"

She turned to face him once more before answering. "Yes."

"Then the position is yours."

She smiled broadly.

"Now, won't you come back and sit down? I'll tell you the particulars."

Caroline gulped down a breath of air. "My lord, if you please, I would rather discuss the details after I have looked at what must be done."

A slight smile flitted across the viscount's features. "I'll have my curricle brought round."

Silence prevailed as the viscount tooled his smart maroon curricle through the streets. Caroline had never ridden in such style before; she ceiling, were solid shelves, row upon row bulging with books. In front of her were three huge windows with white shutters. The wall paneling was painted white, as was all of the woodwork. On the floor was a thick wool carpet of hunter green. Twin crystal chandeliers were suspended from the ceiling, and brass candelabra and wall sconces graced the tables and walls.

Mahogany tables and armchairs were arranged in congenial groups. Against the wall at her back were small escritoires on either side of the entrance. Sofas upholstered in supple, rust-colored leather faced the fireplaces at either end of the room.

"As you can see, no one has ever tried to put these volumes in any sort of order," said the viscount, breaking a long silence.

"Certainly not," agreed Caroline as she moved slowly down the length of the library, shaking her head occasionally as she encountered some beloved work, neglected and forgotten. Finally, she turned back to the viscount. He raised a questioning brow.

"It will take some time, my lord, possibly several months."

"And will you be able to devote such a length of time?"

Caroline paused to consider this last chance to escape, but she knew there was no alternative. Despite the outrageousness of this scheme, she was enjoying London. Besides, she reasoned, they had been in the library for almost an hour, and no member had so much as opened the door. Her work would be solitary for the most part.

She nodded decisively, more to herself than to the viscount.

"Yes, I'll stay until it's finished, my lord."

"And the sum we spoke of . . . will eight hundred pounds be sufficient for your living expenses?"

"Oh, yes, my lord," said Caroline. The sum seemed enormous to her.

His lordship regarded her with doubt. "I think one thousand would be more equitable. London is expensive, and you spoke of your father's house in Cambridge. You'll also want to show a profit of some sort."

Caroline's eyes had widened, but she realized the wisdom of his words and thanked him.

"When do you wish to begin, my boy?" The viscount pronounced the last word deliberately.

"Now. There is no reason to delay."

"Very well, I'll leave you. I'll instruct Boggs to come in here each day at luncheon and tea time. Order what you wish. If you need anything at all, ask Boggs. He's a bit gruff and tends to forget his place at times, but you may rely on him."

"Thank you, my lord," replied Caroline, already pulling books from the shelves at random.

"Do you need help clearing the shelves?"

"I think not, my lord," she said quickly, then gave a rueful grimace. "I prefer to handle this myself."

"As you wish, Pennington," said Rosemeade,

watching for a moment before slipping from the chamber.

Caroline wasted no time in setting to work. She rolled up her sleeves, displaying fine wrists and hands. She eyed the door and shrugged. Surely the dandies who graced White's would think nothing of delicate hands on a young gentleman. After all, the tulips of the ton often applied blanc, a white lead paint, to the backs of their hands.

An hour passed and then another. At the end of this time, Caroline stood back and surveyed the now empty shelves that lined one wall. Manuscripts, bound handwritten letters, and fine leather-bound books littered the floor, stacked in preliminary categories.

First things first, thought Caroline as she wrinkled her nose in disgust at the dusty bookcases. She searched the room for a cloth and found none.

Squaring her shoulders, she swaggered to the door and opened it. A gnarled old footman appeared instantly.

"I'm Boggs, sir. Lord Rosemeade told me to make myself useful to ye."

"Thank you, Boggs. As a matter of fact, I do need some cloths, for cleaning."

"Oh, I'll be 'appy to 'ave someone do that for ye, sir. And if it is convenient, sir, I'll serve yer lunch with 'is lordship's compliments."

"Excellent, Boggs," said Caroline as she pulled out her father's timepiece. "It is later than I thought."

She retreated to the library, picking up a ragged 1710 copy of *The Tatler*. She was soon lost in the intrigues of England of a century before. Boggs entered without a sound, set a tray at her elbow, and then proceeded to supervise the cleaning of the white wooden shelves. He glanced at "his charge," for so the viscount had instructed him to consider the studious young man.

Caroline was brought back to the present as Boggs cleared his throat loudly. She peered up at the old servant. "Have you something to say, Boggs?"

"If ye would prefer something else, sir, I'd be 'appy to bring it to ye."

Caroline chuckled, a delightful sound that caused the footman's scraggly gray brows to rise. "No, Boggs, this is fine. And since the cleaning is finished, I must put aside my reading, have my luncheon, and get back to work. That will be all."

"Just so, sir," said the old man. "Ye need anything else, ye just come to the door. I'll be close by."

Caroline spent the afternoon filling the empty shelves with copies of periodicals such as *The Tatler* and personal journals. This necessitated pulling items from other parts of the library, for they had been tucked here and there, in any nook or cranny.

When Boggs returned to light the candles in the wall sconces, Caroline didn't even look up, she was so absorbed with her task.

wished they could be on the open road, and the horses given their heads.

She surreptitiously studied the handsome face of the man at her side. His chestnut hair and fine gray eyes were compelling, and his straight, aristocratic nose and well-shaped mouth added to his elegant visage. Briefly, Caroline allowed herself to daydream her childhood dream that she was dressed in the latest mode (for a female) and was enjoying popularity in her first season. A dream long cherished, but, as she had always known, impossible for a don's daughter.

Rosemeade's thoughts about his passenger were a mixture of suspicion and amusement. Curiosity had always burned brightly in his character. And here he had been granted an intriguing puzzle to solve, trying to determine Miss Pennington's motives.

He glanced her way. She made an elegant young man with her dark brown locks drawn back in that ridiculously old-fashioned queue. Yes, she would pass muster with the casual observer, though her smooth cheeks and finely arched brows were definitely feminine. Still, the pale complexion could be explained away by pointing to a scholarly disposition and a lifetime spent indoors with books. It would be amusing to see if her disguise would fool the other members at White's. He had always prided himself on his keen observation, but perhaps it had been his remembrance of the youthful Miss Pennington that had made him suspicious. Without this knowledge, would others be as quick to notice her decidedly delicate features? 'Twould be interesting to observe.

"How old are you, Mr. Pennington?" asked the viscount abruptly.

Caroline jumped at his voice. "Twenty, my lord. But, as I said, I worked closely with my father and—"

"I was not questioning your credentials," his lordship said gently.

Caroline stole a quick glance at the viscount's chiseled profile. He felt her gaze and turned slightly, his gray eyes meeting her dark brown ones. Before turning back to his horses, he smiled.

No, thought Caroline. His mouth remained in exactly the same narrow, straight line. But still, she knew he had smiled. It was his eyes, she decided; they lit up, turning a warm blue-gray. Without considering it, Caroline smiled also.

Chapter Two

The library at White's was empty when Viscount Rosemeade led Mr. Pennington inside. Caroline paused and gazed around the vast chamber, trying to digest such overwhelming grandeur.

The walls to her left and right, from floor to

Boggs cleared his throat again. "Ye'll be wantin' yer dinner, sir. Will ye be takin' it in the library?" It was evident from his tone that Boggs knew the answer to his query and disapproved.

"In here," replied Caroline, distracted by his voice.

"Very good, sir," murmured Boggs.

In the corridor, the viscount watched as Boggs passed by. He was shaking his head and muttering under his breath.

"Boggs?"

"What? Oh! It's yer lordship, is it?"

Lord Rosemeade nodded.

"If ye've any influence with yon young gentleman, m'lord, ye'd best be 'aving a talk with 'im. If I'm to look after 'im like a babe—for I swear he's as witless as one—then you'd best tell 'im to eat when I take 'im 'is tray and to quit when I tell 'im it's late."

"He's still working?"

"Working? Lor', I guess so, just about. He had to be scolded to get 'im to stop for a bite o' luncheon, m'lord. Wouldn't stop at all for tea!"

"You should admire such industry, Boggs. Or is it that you're having to work too hard?" teased the viscount.

Boggs snorted. "M'lord, well you know 'ard work never bothered me. And I recall a time when I had to set ye straight about a thing or two, but ye had the good sense to obey me."

"I remember, Boggs, I remember. But you'll just have to be patient with the lad. He'll learn, if you and I can be patient." Rosemeade paused, looking thoughtful. "I suppose there's nothing for it. I must take the young whelp under my wing. For tonight at least. You needn't take Mr. Pennington a tray for dinner, Boggs," he added.

Boggs nodded, satisfied he was leaving his charge in trustworthy hands. After all, it was his lordship's intention to protect the young man from any of the club's unscrupulous or mischievous members; he shouldn't mind taking a hand personally.

Caroline had climbed the movable ladder and was stretching to reach the very top shelf. The viscount paused, enjoying the view of shapely calves and thighs Miss Pennington's raised coat provided.

A slight movement warned Caroline that she was being observed. She quickly lowered her arms; the long skirts of her unfashionable coat dropped down again to cover her limbs.

"Your lordship," she said in surprise. "You needed something? I'm afraid the work I've done has already destroyed what order there was, but I can—"

"No, no, Mr. Pennington. Boggs told me you were still hard at it. You mustn't overtax your strength."

Caroline descended to the floor. "Really, my lord, I've barely done a thing. Working with all this"—she waved a hand around the room—"is hardly work at all. You don't realize what a treasure trove this is, what priceless works rest on these shelves."

At the viscount's raised brow, Caroline blushed.

"That is . . . I'm certain your lordship must . . . I mean . . . you've concerned yourself with—"

A resounding laugh shook the very walls. "Come along, young coxcomb," commanded the viscount.

"Along, my lord?" asked Caroline apprehensively.

"Yes, boy, along." As Caroline hung back, he added with a trace of impatience, "Even one as dedicated as you cannot expect to work till cock's crow."

"Oh, no, my lord, there were just one or two tasks I must complete," Caroline hedged.

Rosemeade regarded the young man for a moment, hands on hips, countenance severe. Suddenly, he sat down.

"Then I'll wait for you."

Caroline opened her mouth to protest but stopped when she saw that it would be futile. She turned, feigning a great interest in a dog-eared copy of Voltaire's *Candide*. A moment later, she gave up and announced that she was ready.

The viscount strode to the door. He held it open, allowing Caroline to pass.

"Where are we going, my lord?"

"Why, to my house, of course. My chef has an excellent way with duck in cassis."

Caroline's eyes grew wide, and her jaw dropped. She quickly hid her reaction, but not before it was noticed by Boggs, who was at that moment entering the corridor.

The footman stepped back into the kitchen. Opening the door a crack, he watched thoughtfully as the two figures receded, the taller one broad-shouldered and manly, the shorter, slim and boyish.

Chapter Three

Shyness enveloped Caroline as she was attended to by two footmen at the viscount's sumptuous table. The first course alone consisted of duck in cassis and soupe à la reine; it was followed by fillets of turbot in garlic, which was accompanied by ham with cranberry sauce, sautéed mushrooms and artichoke hearts, and spinach.

Unaccustomed to such a wide variety, Caroline sampled each dish. As the covers were removed and the next course presented, she found herself feeling fairly stuffed.

"Your chef is indeed very talented, my lord," she commented as the footmen offered her the first tempting dish of the next course, lamb shanks in caper sauce.

"I'm glad you're enjoying your meal, Mr. Pennington. Do have some of the mushroom omelette; it is always excellent."

"Thank you, my lord."

Caroline ate sparingly of the next two courses. She compensated by sipping her wine more often, not wishing to draw attention to her lack of appetite as the viscount continued to enjoy his meal.

As the last course was cleared, Rosemeade said, "Lane, I believe we'll have our port in the library, if you are agreeable, Mr. Pennington."

Caroline nodded her assent and felt the walls begin to spin. She took a deep breath, exhaled slowly, and got to her feet. The movement seemed to steady her, and she managed a sober gait to the library.

Here, the viscount excused himself for a short time. As she strolled about the room, reading titles on the book-lined walls, she felt much better.

"Do you play backgammon, Pennington?" asked the viscount when he returned, a leather case under one arm.

"Indeed, my lord, it is a favorite of mine," she said truthfully.

"I thought it might be." Caroline raised her eyes to his questioningly, and the viscount explained. "The time I visited your father, he taught me to play. Or rather, to enjoy the subtleties of the game, for I had a rough knowledge of it and had boasted of my ability. Needless to say, your father disabused me of any conceit."

Caroline laughed. "My father was never one to

let his opponent win, even if his victim was only just learning the game." In her intoxication, her voice and laugh were high-pitched. The viscount raised a brow in amusement, but Caroline failed to notice.

As they seated themselves at the little table, she asked, "And you also enjoy collecting books, my lord?"

"Yes, I've always been an avid reader, though it is unfashionable to own to such a trait. And since I can never bring myself to part with a volume once I have enjoyed it, my library is rather extensive."

"Do you also garden? I noticed several books on the subject," Caroline commented as she rolled the die.

"No, those were my father's. He was quite a gardener. Most of his books are at Rosemeade. Actually, most of my collection is there also."

"Rosemeade, my lord?"

"My estate near Brighton. You must come down and see it sometime. I have developed my own cataloguing system, though, of course, it is not as elaborate as your father's." The viscount wondered at his own words, but as the night wore on he found it easy to forget her masquerade and treat her like any other acquaintance. No, that was not accurate; it was their shared interest in books that made talking with Miss Pennington so agreeable.

"I'd like very much to see it, my lord," Caroline said as she sipped from the glass of amber liquid Lane had placed at her elbow. Her rehearsals with Livie stood her in good stead, for she felt no rising cough.

The viscount smiled. She was really a very good actress.

For the next three hours Caroline concentrated on the game board while the viscount concentrated on observing her. He told himself he was doing her a disservice by allowing her to continue with her impossible masquerade. Still, he was enjoying the game and the conversation and could not bring himself to expose his guest's ruse. Not yet, he told himself sternly.

Caroline gave as good as she got, though the last few games were a blur to her. The port flowed freely, and it was not until she rose to leave that the books around her began to spin and she grabbed the table to steady herself.

"Seems a bit . . ." she muttered.

"Yes, my dear, and I fear tomorrow may be quite unpleasant. Let me help you."

Afraid he could detect her softness, Caroline managed to stand unaided but stumbled on her way to the door. Two strong arms caught her; she found her befuddled gaze on the viscount as she turned in his embrace. His face only inches from hers, Rosemeade quelled an absurd impulse to kiss her tempting lips.

"My carriage is waiting at the door; my coachman will see you home safely," said his lordship quietly.

"Much obliged, m'lor'," Caroline managed with great effort, and she cautiously walked out into the cool night.

"Take it easy with our guest, John," the viscount softly instructed his coachman. With a chuckle, the old man nodded and gently closed the coach door.

"Olivia, it's me . . . uh, I. Are you awake?" whispered Caroline loudly.

The door flew open; Olivia dragged her young friend into her bedchamber and shut the door.

"Where have you been, young lady? I've been pacing this floor for the past five hours!" Miss Stanton shook her finger under Caroline's nose.

Caroline smiled stupidly at her small, indignant friend.

"Caroline, stop gawking and tell me what has happened."

"Nothin', Livie. Nothin' at all."

"Caroline Pennington!" exclaimed Olivia, standing on tiptoe in front of her former charge. "You are disguised!"

"Devil a bit, Livie," she mumbled.

Olivia pursed her lips, her eyes narrowing with determination. "Caroline, sit down."

Caroline complied. "Really, Livie, I'm perfectly able—"

"No doubt, miss. But you will sit here until I can loosen this cravat and remove this binding. Where is your nightshirt?"

Caroline essayed a nonchalant shrug that looked coarse, uneven.

Olivia eyed her askance. "Stay put while I go and find it."

When Olivia returned, she found her long-legged charge curled into a tight ball, her head resting on the arm of the overstuffed chair, her knees nearly touching her strong chin. Olivia smoothed the dark brown curls that had escaped from the neat queue.

"Such a desperate escapade, little one," she murmured before grasping the younger woman's wrists and pulling her into a sitting position.

"No, Livie," whined Caroline.

"Oh, yes, young lady. Now you sit up like a good girl while I get you into this nightshirt."

Tucked up in her own bed, Caroline thanked Olivia sleepily and closed her eyes.

"Sleep well, my dear. I fear your morning will not be so peaceful," said Olivia with a knowing smile.

Miss Stanton's prophecy proved too true. At first, Caroline could not remember where she was; that was not surprising, for her eyes refused to open. Her arms and legs were filled with lead. She tried to swallow and couldn't. She heard a door open somewhere, though ears and mind could not agree on the origin of the sound.

"Caroline, dear," whispered Olivia.

"Ach, Livie, I've been drugged." She moaned, her own voice resounding as though she were inside a huge bell with her head as the clapper, crashing back and forth.

"No, Caroline, you have not been drugged, precisely. You are merely experiencing the result of an evening spent carousing about London."

Caroline sat up suddenly. "I was not carousing! I was only . . . Oh! Livie, my head hurts so!" She gasped.

Miss Stanton placed a cool damp cloth on Caroline's head. Then she rearranged the blanket and tiptoed to the door, leaving her charge to her solitary misery.

"If you need anything, my dear," she said quietly at the door.

A weak wave of three fingers motioned her away.

Viscount Rosemeade dressed with care for his morning call on his new employee. As he tied his cravat, he thought of his old professor, and in his mind's eye flashed back to that visit so many years before when a bright-eyed, dark-haired girl had burst into Pennington's library. She had been a gawky, long-legged thing who had sketched a hasty curtsy his way before plunging headlong into her tale. Her name, he recalled the professor saying proudly, was Caroline, after his first name, Charles.

So he was faced with a perplexing problem. If this was Professor Pennington's daughter, what was her game? Had she fallen into bad times or bad company? Was she doing this for a lark? Or —and he hated to consider it—was she no better than numerous other young "ladies" who had attempted to force him into marriage by compromising themselves in his company? After all, he had known many honorable men who had produced scheming, self-serving offspring.

Whatever her reason, he reflected grimly as he stepped from his curricle, he would have the answer before he left.

"It is good of you to receive me, Mrs. Stanton," said the viscount as he seated himself opposite his hostess. He was intrigued by her neat appearance; indeed, by the proper and upright demeanor of the entire household. There appeared to be nothing havey-cavey about it.

"Not at all, my lord," replied Olivia Stanton. "I assume you've come to inquire about my nephew since he is not at his post today."

Deciding to play along, Rosemeade said, "Yes, though you mustn't imagine that I fault him for that, ma'am." He flashed her his most winning smile but was rewarded by only a slight curl of her lips. He cleared his throat, wondering how this small lady, who was of an age with him, could render him so discomfited.

"I'm afraid you are a bit put out with me, Mrs. Stanton, over last evening. I assure you, I had no idea the, uh, lad was so susceptible to port."

"He has never before indulged in such diversions, my lord," she responded.

The viscount shifted uncomfortably on the edge of his chair. "I see."

A long pause ensued.

"Well, then, I must personally apologize to Mr. Pennington. I want to assure him that I consider myself responsible."

"That will not be possible today, my lord. My nephew is far too weak to be disturbed," said

Miss Stanton firmly. She stood up, hoping to give the viscount his cue to depart.

But Robert Wyndridge, Viscount Rosemeade, was not the man to be turned once he had reached a decision. He would not leave without seeing Miss Pennington. He rose, towering over Olivia, his presence not menacing but immovable.

"I don't think you understand, Mrs. Stanton, if that is truly your name. I wish to speak to your companion, and I shan't leave until I do."

Olivia toyed with the idea of calling the butler but dismissed the thought. If Bates were present, it might be different, but Biggers was a stranger. And if the game was up, then perhaps it was for the best, she concluded philosophically.

"Come this way, my lord." Livie led the way to Caroline's bedroom, having decided any confrontation would be best gotten over with in private.

"Wait here, please," she said with great dignity.

Insane! thought the viscount. I am insane to allow myself to be forced into such a compromising situation! But even as this thought occurred to him, he dismissed it. Somehow, he could not believe it of Miss Pennington. Then Miss Stanton returned to lead him into the darkened chamber.

Caroline was propped up on pillows; her head ached and she was fighting down panic at the prospect of this encounter.

"My lord," she began weakly. "Please be seated. I hope you'll forgive my not rising."

The viscount nodded, impressed by her composure. She appeared a veritable child in her man's nightshirt. He set a straight-backed chair close to the bed. Miss Stanton stood at the head of the bed, positioning herself as a dog does between its master and an intruder.

"I have come today to apologize for aiding in your discomfort, and, I must admit, to satisfy my own curiosity as to your true identity and intention."

Caroline managed to look dignified despite her very undignified position. She reminded the viscount of his first visit from the mysterious Mr. Pennington.

"I shall satisfy your curiosity first, my lord. I am Charles Pennington, only child of the late Professor Charles Pennington."

"You mean, only daughter."

Caroline took a resigned breath; it had been an unlikely undertaking. "Yes," she said simply. The effort seemed to drain the last of her defiant pride, and she felt tears of self-pity spring forth. She swallowed hard and willed herself to remain calm.

"How could you possibly have expected this impersonation to succeed?"

"Livie, leave us."

"I won't! Caroline, you—"

"Don't worry, madam. I shan't forget I'm a gentleman; word of a Wyndridge." Olivia hesitated but a moment before melting from the room.

Caroline began slowly. "You ask how I could hope to succeed, my lord. I ask you, circumstanced as I have been, how could I not at least try? Poverty is not a pleasant prospect, but when you know your dearest friend and retainers will also be forced into destitution, you become desperate, grasping at any straws, however mad. And this"—she waved a hand toward her nightshirt—"this was the best." She gave a bitter laugh, causing the dull ache in her temples to sharpen.

"So you came to London to make your fortune."

The pain in her head had traveled to the region of her heart, and Caroline struggled to sit up straight, determined to justify herself to this virtual stranger.

"In order to have food, I was going to sell my father's house. I was at the point of dismissing the Bateses, who have served me all my life. I knew it unlikely they could find other positions at their stage of life. My dear friend Olivia, who has been more like a mother, was to share my fate. Then your letter came; it was like a sign. But how can you possibly understand? You, a viscount, a Wyndridge of Rosemeade."

Caroline was on her feet now, ignoring the pain as she looked the viscount in the eye. All the fear and hopelessness of the past year poured forth in her words and tones.

Rosemeade studied her face, reading the pain

and frustration there. It was like peering into a soul, and he heard a voice speaking and realized it was his own.

"You needn't worry any longer, Caroline. Your secret is safe with me. For now, get back into that bed and go to sleep." And he proceeded to tuck in his stunned "clerk." Then he left the room.

The viscount nodded curtly to Miss Stanton as he left the chamber. Livie, wide-eyed with surprise, scurried after him as he descended the stairs. He stopped short near the front door and turned to face her.

"I must think, Mrs. Stanton. Tell—" He spied Biggers in time and continued more discreetly. "I'll expect to see him at White's first thing in the morning."

"Why, thank you, my lord," stammered Olivia, curtsying.

He returned an elegant bow, which drew a smile from his bewildered hostess.

"I do want to thank you for sending Charles home in your carriage last night. That was most considerate."

" 'Twas the least I could do. I could see the 'boy' was past caring."

Miss Stanton could not prevent the glimmer of amusement from creeping into her eyes. The viscount merely said, "Exactly," as a footman let him out.

"Good evening, Livie," said Caroline through clenched teeth.

"Why, Charles, I hardly expected to see you

up and about this evening," Miss Stanton exclaimed as she entered the dining salon.

"Shh. Please, Aunt Olivia. Quietly. My head still aches."

"If I were a lesser person, I would content myself with a 'serves you right.'"

"But, of course, you'll not stoop so low," murmured Caroline.

"Of course not, dear. Yes, Biggers, I should love some scalloped breast of chicken. It smells divine."

Caroline blanched and quickly waved the footman away. She nibbled at a buttered roll and sipped her water with caution.

"You haven't told me yet how you found the library at White's. I assumed since you and his lordship were so 'involved' last night that all went well?"

"Yes, Aunt Olivia. I worked all morning and afternoon until the viscount dragged me away."

"Dragged you?"

Caroline noted Biggers's interested air and turned the topic until they had finished their meal. Once they were alone, Olivia demanded an explanation.

"I don't know why, but the viscount wanted me to dine with him. My show of reluctance didn't deter him, so I had to agree," said Caroline.

"Do you think he knew then?"

Caroline shook her head. "Suspected, perhaps. What did he say after he left me this morning?"

"Only that he would see you at White's in the morning."

"It would seem he intends to let me go on with the work," said Caroline hopefully.

"So it seems. But, my dear, I do hope you'll be careful. He's a very powerful man; don't underestimate him."

Conversation ceased while Biggers entered with the tea tray. As soon as the butler left them, Olivia poured a cup of strong tea for Caroline. A deep drink seemed to jog her memory, and she began to describe her first day enthusiastically.

"Livie, you wouldn't believe all the fascinating volumes and papers. I read a portion of the personal journal of a man named Greville, probably some relation to the Grenvilles."

"At the viscount's house?"

"No, no, at White's, though I will tell you about the viscount's library also. Anyway, this Greville spent two years on a pirate ship in the French Indies at the turn of the century."

"Was it a journal or a novel?" asked Olivia in disbelief.

"A journal, without doubt. If not, he had quite a talent for fiction."

"Caroline, how long will it take you to catalogue the entire collection?"

"Some time, I fear. Two months, possibly more."

"Good heavens! I'd no idea! But that means . . . Shall we have time when we return home to set everything to rights before the fall term begins?"

"I believe so. I shall try very hard merely to catalogue and not to read everything on the shelves," Caroline replied.

Finally, Olivia posed the question she had so long withheld.

"What do you think of Viscount Rosemeade?"

Caroline reddened. "What did you think, Livie?"

"He seemed quite handsome. But, of course, I didn't see him long."

"He really is quite charming, Livie," Caroline revealed at length. "I was afraid he might try to become involved in the actual cataloguing. And as you know, I prefer to work alone. But although he asked how things were going, he didn't dwell on it. And he was an excellent host."

"What did you find to talk about all evening?"

"All manner of things, Livie. We played backgammon and talked about literature in general, Bonaparte and the war, opera—all manner of things."

Miss Stanton smiled indulgently but could not resist a teasing query. "I thought he would be older, didn't you?" she asked.

"I suppose."

"He has very fine eyes. Blue, aren't they?"

"No, gray."

"Hmm. And then of course his bearing, so tall and muscular. Quite a handsome figure, don't you think?"

"I suppose." Caroline caught the amused gleam in Olivia's eyes and made a face. "Really,

Olivia, I had too much on my mind to judge the viscount personally!"

"Very well," answered Olivia, a smile breaking forth. "So what else did you talk about?"

"His library, at his home."

"Was it impressive?"

"Was it imp— Oh, no, not here in London, at his country house near Brighton, Rosemeade. Oh, yes! He insists I must learn to ride."

"To ride?" exclaimed Olivia "What on earth for?"

Caroline laughed at her friend's incredulous expression. "Because, my dear Livie, his lordship says I must have the loan of a horse while in London. When I replied that I didn't ride, he nearly choked on his Brussels sprout."

"And that made you agree to this ill-advised scheme?"

"Not precisely." Caroline paused, taking time suddenly to explore her motives for agreeing to the viscount's offer. She shook her head very slowly. "I'm not certain why I agreed. I suppose I feared he might suspect something if I told him how I really feel about horses." She shrugged. "But now I shan't have to worry about that."

"And if he insists? How will you manage?"

"I shall simply have to hide my dislike of the beasts."

"You won't be able to. A horse can sense fear," objected Livie.

"Oh, nonsense. Besides, I don't fear them; I just don't trust them. You never know what they're going to do next."

* * *

Caroline boldly repeated these same words to the viscount the next morning when he arrived to pull her away from her work once more. She could envision the years stretching on as she labored to catalogue the library.

"Then let's be off," Rosemeade said cheerfully.

"But, my lord, I have work to do. Work for which you hired me. Work with which I need to proceed."

"Perhaps, but I wish to be private with you, and an hour out in the morning sun will benefit you greatly. You'll return ready to move mountains—of books, that is."

"I doubt it," mumbled Caroline as she picked up her hat and followed the viscount out the door and down White's front steps.

She stopped short when she saw the two horses waiting at the curb. Both were over sixteen hands high; the viscount strode up to one and took the reins from Henry, his groom.

Looking down, he inquired, "Surely you can mount."

Caroline jumped, swallowed hard, and nodded. The groom still held her horse's bridle. She gathered the reins, speaking softly to the beast. It swung its head around, eyeing her malevolently.

"That's it, my pretty nag," she whispered sweetly. "You would be considered a tasty meal in France," she added. The horse whickered.

Placing one foot in the stirrup and grasping the pommel, she pulled herself up, slowly swinging her right leg across and placing that foot firmly in its stirrup. It was as she breathed a sigh of relief and managed a grimace of a smile for the viscount that the animal decided to taste her leg.

"Ouch!" she yelped, and lashed out to kick the beast's nose. But he was too quick for her; catching her off balance, he jumped to the right and then crab-stepped daintily back to the left. Caroline tumbled to the ground.

"Ho! Pennington! I say, are you hurt?" asked the viscount.

She glared up at him and said through clenched teeth, "Not at all, my lord. It's the quickest way to dismount, don't you think? I only wish I'd known I wanted to dismount," she added as the big horse bent his head to her knees and gave her a nudge.

"I'm getting up," she informed the horse. "If I am able, you beast," she grumbled.

Rosemeade doubled up with laughter; the groom was half lying on the steps of the club, his mirth uncontrollable.

"I'm sorry, Pennington, truly I am. Assumed you could handle old Skipper," said the viscount, his voice still quivering.

Caroline muttered, "I bet you did. What did you call this flea-bitten apparition, my lord?"

"Skipper. I've had him forever; must be at least fifteen. Can you remount?"

"Hold his head, you," she commanded the groom. "And if you let go, my good man, I shall throw you!"

The groom grinned but pulled his forelock

most respectfully and held the big horse firmly as Caroline remounted without mishap.

"We'll ride to the park. It's so early, we may be the only ones there. Skipper can be a bit stubborn at times, but he's a good horse for an inexperienced rider. He knows to lead with his right, and his trot is so rough, you'll post in self-defense."

"How comforting," commented Caroline dryly.

The viscount spoke the truth. A half-hour of Skipper's jolting trot and Caroline was posting beautifully. Her legs were trembling with the effort. She reflected that though her backside was not bruised, her legs would be so sore she wouldn't be able to move by morning.

Pulling off the well-trodden path, the viscount led the way to a clearing and dismounted. He went to Skipper's head and grasped the bridle while Caroline slipped to the ground.

Rosemeade indicated a huge stump where Caroline sat down while he leaned against a tree and regarded her in silence. She began to fidget with her coat buttons as he seemed frozen in contemplation.

Finally he spoke, but his words surprised her.

"You are staying at Penn Wickersham's. A relative?"

"Yes, my first cousin. He let me have his house for the summer."

"How do you manage to fool the servants?"

"I suppose they are not so different from us.

They don't seem to notice us any more than we do them."

The viscount snorted. "Rubbish! They notice everything! And most of it travels from one servants' hall to the next. If that butler hasn't guessed the whole, I should be very surprised."

Caroline's eyes flashed, but she retained control, merely replying tightly, "It's of no matter, my lord. The entire staff is going on holiday as soon as my own servants arrive."

"When will that be?"

"Tomorrow."

"You realize if you are discovered in this masquerade, you will be ruined. And don't think word will not spread back to Cambridge."

"I'm prepared to face the consequences."

"And your aunt?"

"She agrees."

"One thing more, so there will be no further misunderstanding. I sent my lawyer to Cambridge yesterday to learn what he could about your circumstances. It seems you told me the truth."

"Of course!" Caroline exclaimed indignantly.

The viscount held up his hand to cut short her protestations. "You forget, my dear Miss Pennington, I have reason to know you're not always scrupulously honest."

Caroline had no reply to this, but her chest swelled with injured pride.

"You see, I must be cautious. At risk of sounding immodest, I am considered a matrimonial prize, and a number of young ladies have gone to very peculiar lengths to entice me to the altar."

"How fortunate for them they failed," Caroline snapped. She realized her impetuous tongue had betrayed her again.

But the viscount, once he had recovered from his surprise, gave a shout of laughter.

"You're a sharp-tongued baggage, aren't you?"

He watched her intently for a moment longer before sighing and walking over to face her. He extended his hand, and Caroline took it timidly. Pulling her to her feet, he persisted in holding her hand captive, his thumb rubbing her palm and causing her breathing to quicken.

"You may continue at White's," he began, but was interrupted by Caroline's exclamation of gratitude.

"Let me finish," he added. Caroline folded her arms to keep her hands from fluttering. "I intend to impose several conditions. You will follow my instructions or face immediate dismissal."

The final word sobered Caroline, and she subsided to the stump as her knees grew weak.

"First, as soon as your own servants arrive, you will cease wearing men's clothing when you're at home."

Caroline nodded obediently.

"You will not go out in society dressed as a man."

"That shouldn't be a problem. I have no acquaintances in society, anyway."

"Nevertheless, there'll be no trips to the opera, theater, or sightseeing dressed as you now are."

"Yes, my lord," she replied.

"And no more, shall we say, indulging in spirits."

Caroline closed her eyes, nodding fervently.

"Furthermore, Henry, my groom, will see you home every evening, or you will take a hackney."

"Really, my lord, I hardly think it necessary. It is not that far."

"But you will agree," he insisted.

"Yes," she grumbled. "I agree to the hackney. I expect my hours will be too irregular to keep your groom so occupied."

It was his turn to nod.

"Is that all?"

"One more thing, Miss Pennington. I think to protect this masquerade, you will become Charles Pennington at White's, brother of Miss Caroline Pennington. When I meet you in your guise as Charles, I shall address you as Mr. Pennington, my boy, etc., even when we are alone. And Mr. Charles Pennington will be something of a recluse, rarely showing his face anywhere at White's except for the library. Agreed?"

"Yes, my lord," replied Caroline. "Now, I suppose we can forget these ridiculous riding lessons."

The viscount's handsome gray eyes lit with a boyish twinkle.

"Certainly not. Everyone should know how to ride, especially a young man such as yourself!"

With a groan, Caroline followed him to the horses and remounted without enthusiasm.

* * *

As the pair reentered White's, Caroline noticed there were more members present. Many gentlemen of London evidently liked to escape from their homes before noon. She smiled; it was rather like a henpecked haven.

"*Cher* Rosemeade!" exclaimed a tall, weasel-faced gentleman as he caught sight of the viscount.

"Épernon," the viscount acknowledged him with a brisk nod.

"I have been away so long, I fear you would have forgotten me," gushed the other man, his narrow eyes darting from the viscount to the young man at his side.

"Not likely, Épernon. What do you want?"

"Want? Why, *rien du tout, mon vieux;* nothing at all. Merely to renew our friendship. But come, you do not introduce me to your young comrade."

Rosemeade grimaced but complied. "Armand Pichette, le comte d'Épernon; Mr. Charles Pennington."

The viscount was so sharp, Caroline looked up in surprise. Obviously, there was no love lost between him and the comte.

Looking down at Caroline, the viscount almost laughed aloud at her expression of awe. This desire vanished as he noticed the comte's calculating visage and heard his smooth words.

"*Enchanté, mon jeune homme;* ah! my lamentable memory. I should say, my dear young man, *n'est-ce pas?*"

"Ce n'est pas nécessaire, monsieur le comte. Je comprends le français."

"Ah, Rosemeade! How wonderful of you to introduce me to such a charming companion. What a delight to find someone so conversant with my native tongue. We must have many long talks, you and I, Monsieur Pennington."

Caroline was prevented from answering as the viscount cut her off. "That will be impossible. Mr. Pennington is in my employ and is far too occupied to socialize, Épernon. Good day."

With this, Rosemeade stalked off, leaving Caroline no choice but to follow, her face crimson with anger and humiliation.

Without a word, she began to work on the shelves, not actually accomplishing anything but alleviating her exasperation. The viscount leaned against the door, silently debating whether he should offer an apology. Miss Pennington's pride once again, he thought impatiently.

"Mr. Pennington," he whispered. When the books continued to be shuffled, he said with more force, "Charles, perhaps I owe you an explanation."

Caroline turned, her brown eyes dark with fury. She sat down abruptly, arms akimbo, shoulders squared. The viscount's eyes lighted though his expression did not alter. He went to take a seat opposite his employee.

"You may have misinterpreted my comments out there."

"That is doubtful, my lord. I only wonder that

you waste your valuable time in the company of an employee. Surely you have a bet to place, a coat to order, or . . . or a rout to attend!"

Even as the words left her mouth, Caroline stifled a gasp. The fire in her own eyes was doused by his lordship's disdainful glare. She struggled to meet his gaze but found she could not. Her eyes dropped to her hands; she didn't realize he had left the room until the door clicked shut in his wake.

Almost in a daze, she arose and began sorting through stacks of books: three in French, two novels, a Latin textbook, a tattered copy of Johnson's dictionary.

"Excuse me, sir."

"What is it, Boggs?" said Caroline in surprise.

"I've brought ye some tea, sir, since you didn't order any luncheon."

Caroline pulled out her watch, noting in amazement that it was past four in the afternoon. Where had the time gone? She sat down abruptly, and Boggs placed the tray in front of her. He waited a moment, then as she made no motion to pour out, he lifted the small pot and handed it to her firmly. Caroline accepted it without a word and the servant walked away.

Boggs had witnessed the viscount's angry departure; he had seen that same look countless times when serving in the Peninsula with Major Wyndridge. It generally meant there was a victim of his anger somewhere close by.

Taking pity on his new "charge," Boggs said quietly, " 'is lordship 'as a temper, Mr. Pennington, and he ain't used to anyone crossing 'im, don't ye see. But I've never known 'im to turn on a body and use 'is power to get even-like."

At first he was uncertain whether the young man had heard him, but gradually he saw the stiff shoulders relax. Thoughtful eyes met the old servant's, understanding and acceptance dawning in their depths.

"Thank you, Boggs," Caroline whispered.

"Of course."

Caroline perched on a footstool, sifting through the text of a worn volume of Latin. The cover and title page were missing, and she was trying to determine its origin. It seemed to be a journal, but she was unfamiliar with the writings. The morning sun streamed through the slanted louvers of the window shutters, lighting her fine profile.

A deep voice intruded. "You'll go blind reading in this light, Mr. Pennington. Let me open those shutters for you."

Caroline colored at being found in such a ridiculous posture. Ah, well, she reasoned, a man may sit where and how he pleases, and she was dressed for the part.

His lordship had turned and was regarding her with curiosity. "I hope you're not still angry over that incident," began the viscount, mistaking her embarrassment for anger.

She rose to face him. "No, my lord, as I hope

you are not." Her need to explain grew as she regarded his concerned face, a stray lock of hair falling boyishly across his forehead. She longed to reach out and brush it aside, to touch his smooth forehead.

"Certainly not, my boy. But I do want to . . . to explain my words."

Caroline shook her head, returning from her reverie, and raised her hand to halt his speech.

"It is I who owe you an apology for my impertinence. That is, I had no reason to speak so rudely to you, my lord," she said, a delightful blush spreading over her features once again.

"I know you had no reason," said his lordship, "but you didn't know that. What I mean is, I was not saying you were unsuitable company for the comte d'Épernon, but that he would be unsuitable for you. Suffice it to say, the man's a rogue."

Her reply was hesitant. "If you say so, my lord. Though I must say, he seemed a gentleman."

The viscount snorted. "Allow that I'm the better judge in the matter, my, uh, boy, and have nothing further to do with Épernon."

"I shall not seek him out, my lord, but in my position, it would not do to give him the cut direct."

One brow rose at this, but the viscount had wearied of the the subject and let it drop. "Come along now, Pennington," he said, and strode toward the door.

"Where, my lord?" Caroline inquired with a sinking feeling.

"For our riding lesson, of course. You didn't think I'd forgotten," he answered, laughing, as he went out the door.

"Of course not," she grumbled. "I couldn't be so fortunate."

This lesson was going a little better. At least old Skipper hadn't managed to bite her or to throw her yet. Instead, she moaned inwardly, the beast had decided to shake her to death. True, his rough gait did cause her to remember to post. One moment of forgetfulness left her feeling bruised and beaten.

The viscount sometimes spoke a word of encouragement; otherwise, he remained silent.

As they slowed to a walk, Caroline commented, "The weather has been lovely the past few days."

Rosemeade looked at her for the first time. "Have I reduced you to making conversation about the weather?"

"The weather has always been the mainstay of English conversation."

"But it is normally used to initiate conversation. You must forgive my neglecting you."

"Perhaps you would prefer to return to the club, my lord."

"You would, I feel certain. However, I shan't be selfish, and you are doing much better today."

"Thank you, my lord." She flashed him a smile. "Nevertheless, I'll understand if you have other business."

"No, not business. A personal matter."

"I see."

"It is my brother who was with Wellesley in the Peninsula."

"Was?"

"It has been several months since I heard from him, and the Home Office refuses to tell me where he is."

"Why?"

He shrugged. "Too many leaks already."

"Leaks?"

"There are those who hope to gain financially in this war. They are not particular about who the victor may be."

Caroline's eyes widened. "Spies?"

"Don't worry," he whispered, "I daresay you are safe in the library at White's."

After reaching the safety of the library, she gingerly rubbed the offended portion of her body.

"Do you enjoy a ride on horseback, *monsieur*? Horses are such uncomfortable creatures, *n'est-ce pas?*"

Caroline's head jerked up, startled to hear the comte's voice intruding in her little sanctuary.

"I apologize; I have frightened you," Épernon said, his smile not reaching his eyes.

"No, *monsieur*. It is just that there is rarely anyone in here but myself. Were you looking for something?"

"Yes, I was. But it was nothing of import. Not vital, as you English say. You are not from London, I believe?"

"No, *monsieur*. Cambridge is my home, just east of here."

"And this is your first visit to London?"

"My first extended visit. I have been here briefly before," she answered.

"Hmm. It seems odd to me—though, of course, I am but an *émigré*—that a young man would choose to spend all his time here, with books, when there are countless other attractions awaiting him."

Caroline stiffened slightly. Was this what the viscount meant about Epernon's being a rogue? Did he lure unsuspecting, green youths to financial ruin? She had heard her father speak of the infamous gambling hells in Pall Mall. She listened warily as the comte continued.

"I know any number of young ladies who would delight in having such a handsome young man at their routs."

Caroline relaxed again. So that was the "attraction" he spoke about! Leave it to a Frenchman, she thought. If he only knew! She could have laughed outright at the thought, but the comte's scrutiny continued.

Trying to allay any suspicion, she said, "I am but an employee of the viscount. I am not in London to indulge in frivolity, and I doubt whether those young ladies would entertain such a penniless prize as myself."

"Ah, you are too harsh, my young friend. *Les femmes?* What do they care? A handsome face, a graceful bow, eh?"

"If you say so, *monsieur*," replied Caroline, her

eyes drifting longingly to the Latin journal, which lay beside the stool where she had left it.

The comte took his cue. "Ah, well, I have too long kept you from your work, *mon ami. Au revoir.*"

The strange interview thus terminated, Caroline returned to her duties, but she spared a stray thought for Armand Pichette. An *émigré*, he had said; probably escaped the Terror with only the shirt on his back. Driven from his home—she could readily identify with that! A bit talkative, but not wrapped up in his own problems, she thought. No doubt lonely, too. I don't care what the viscount says, she decided. I will speak to Épernon if I please. There can be no harm in that.

Rain swept through London that night. Not a gentle summer rain, but a hard, demanding downpour that washed the gutters of even the filthiest streets in the slums. Coaches were scarce; pedestrians nonexistent.

But the pelting drops of rain failed to deter two determined individuals who met at the entrance to the park behind the gates, away from any prying eyes.

They exchanged few words though the average passerby could not have understood the language, much less have repeated it to any interested authorities. A scroll was exchanged, and they separated.

As Épernon reached the street, a coach—that of a nobleman by the elaborate crest on the door

—passed through the gates, and he jumped back quickly, forgetting to duck in his surprise.

"Strange."

"What, Robert?"

"That looked like . . . Oh, never mind, Ferdie. Nothing important."

"How is your work proceeding, Caroline?" asked Olivia that same evening.

Caroline let the curtain drop across the rain-spattered windowpanes and turned slowly. "Very well, I suppose."

"That's good, dear," Olivia said, wondering at her charge's restless state. She laid aside her embroidery frame and walked to the ivory and ebony chess set on the other side of the room.

"Would you care for a game, Caroline? I must confess to being a bit bored with my own company this evening."

Caroline repented immediately. "Of course, Aunt; I fear I've not been company to you at all of late."

Livie smiled at the "aunt." Since they had decided she was to portray—for propriety's sake—young Mr. Pennington's widowed aunt, Caroline had taken to calling her by that appellation even when they were alone. It seemed quite natural, though "mother" might have been even more appropriate.

They played in silence—check, countercheck, checkmate. Olivia exclaimed in delight as she claimed Caroline's king.

"Now I know you're distracted! I never win unless something is troubling you."

Caroline's lopsided grin broke forth. "I knew there was a reason I shouldn't accept your challenge."

Olivia rose from the chess table, placed her hand on Caroline's head, and stroked the short curls gently. Prying was not in her nature. "I believe I'll retire now, dear."

"What? Before the tea tray, Livie?"

Olivia smiled brightly and ran her hands down her shapely hips. "I'm afraid the cuisine here in London suits me only too well! However, I don't intend to return home wearing it!" She strolled from the room, leaving Caroline alone with her thoughts.

These were not comfortable. She wandered to and fro, bending to sniff the flowers in the vase on the table, inspecting—though not seeing—Olivia's embroidery stitches, tracing the rivulets of rain on the windowpane, and finally forcing herself to sit in front of the fire simulating a tranquillity she could not feel.

But why? she asked herself. Why should she feel so restless? Her tottering finances had been steadied. Her masquerade had been detected, but she felt comfortable with the result. She was enjoying the task she had undertaken. The men she met at White's were unexceptionable: Boggs, the comte, a silly youth named Willie Needham, and an old man whose off-color jokes made her blush. All was quite satisfactory. And the viscount . . .

The Scandalous Miss

Is what? she asked herself. Is a pleasant man, came the rational answer. He's also very intelligent; she had discovered that during their rides. He's generous, too. And undoubtedly the most handsome man she'd ever met, she added.

At this, Caroline's head jerked up; her eyes flitted from one side to the other as though to spy some eavesdropper on her thoughts. She gave a jerky little laugh and then retreated to the window as though the cleansing rain could wash away her frightening daydreams.

This is all nonsense, she resolved. I am not a fool. Any woman would find Rosemeade attractive, with his chestnut hair, strong jaw, straight nose, and those speaking gray eyes. He wore his clothes casually, though his coats fit like a glove. His breeches fit his thighs . . . Nonsense!

Caroline said to herself firmly, I am a well brought up lady, and would never throw myself at a man's feet, no matter how impetuous I am. There is no reason to even suspect I would do such an absurd thing with the viscount!

She laughed out loud at the thought.

Ridiculous!

The rain continued into the next morning, but Lord Rosemeade was oblivious to it as he hurried into White's.

"Good morning, Boggs."

"Good mornin', m'lord."

"Is our young charge here?"

"Yes, m'lord. He's been hard at it since before I

arrived. He did stop for mornin' tea, though, so I don't think he's too involved."

"Good heavens, man! I don't care if he's taken his tea or not. I'm not his mother!"

No aristocrat could have shown more haughty disdain than Boggs as he raised his scraggly gray brows. But he uttered not a word.

The viscount grimaced and stalked past the old servant, grumbling about impertinence, old dogs, and young puppies.

When the door opened, Caroline looked up; she wondered for a second if she had conjured him. Absurd! she chided herself, and determined to be civil but not friendly.

This was not a difficult task, for the viscount was in no mood for pleasantries himself.

"My lord," Caroline said by way of greeting.

"Pennington, I shall be out of the city for a time," he said, then paused.

"Yes, my lord?" she prompted.

"I shan't be here to advise you or to give you your riding lessons," he explained.

What a relief, she wanted to say. Instead, she observed coolly, "I hardly expected to ride today, my lord."

In his exasperation, the viscount's mouth dropped open, snapped closed, and then opened again. He regarded his employee with suspicion, but Caroline's expression remained impassive. He relaxed slightly and then noticed the innocent brown eyes that gazed back at him.

"Young jackanapes!" he exclaimed. Gray eyes

and brown locked, and simultaneously the pair dissolved into laughter.

When they had both recovered, the viscount cocked his head to one side and said, "I should throw you out into the rain for your impudence. 'Twould be an easy task, you know."

"Perhaps, my lord, but I wager you'd not come out of the encounter unscathed." She faced him, legs braced, ready to defend herself.

A banty rooster, he thought, that's what the chit looks like standing there dressed in men's finery. He grinned at this thought.

Caroline relaxed and offered her benefactor some tea.

"No, I can't stay. I'm off to Rosemeade to see my latest acquisition."

"What's that, my lord?"

"A stallion, Holier Than Thou." At Caroline's puzzled look, he added, "I bought him for breeding purposes at my estate."

"But how is it you haven't seen your acquisition before now?"

"But I have. At least I did once, two years ago at the races. Anyway, Farningham made the purchase."

"Your agent?" asked Caroline.

"Farningham? I should hope not! I'd find myself owner of half the horseflesh in England!" He shuddered. "No, no. Farningham is a very good friend who recommended I buy Mallory's stud."

As Caroline seemed to be waiting for more of an explanation, he continued, "You must know, breeding horses is a hobby of mine, but I can't keep up with it like Farningham. To me, it is a pastime; to Ferdie, it is a passion."

"So he offers you advice."

"Exactly!" exclaimed his lordship, relieved to be finished with the irksome topic.

"The horse is at Rosemeade, my lord?" Caroline asked.

"Yes," he answered, noting her longing tone when she said Rosemeade. Of course, he thought, she wishes to see my library. Impulsively, he extended the invitation.

"Oh, no, my lord," Caroline almost yelped. "I couldn't think of intruding! That is, it is very gracious of you, but I have my work to do here."

Though not disappointed, her refusal intrigued him. He said, "Your aunt, too, of course."

"No, my lord."

"But surely a few days . . ."

"No, I could not."

"Very well, Pennington. You know best, I'm sure."

"I do thank you," said Caroline, trying to keep the wistful note from her voice.

The viscount waved her gratitude aside and prepared to leave. He paused at the door.

"By the way, Henry will deliver a hack each morning at ten, weather permitting, so that you may continue your rides. Good-bye."

"Ah! Monsieur Pennington, what good fortune! I did not expect to find you here at this time of the morning. You are usually with Rosemeade at this hour, *n'est-ce pas?*"

"*Bonjour, monsieur le comte.* The viscount has been out of town for several days," she replied.

Since she was glancing at the book in her hand, Caroline failed to notice the speculative gleam that sprang to life in the comte's eyes.

"So, you are deprived of your benefactor's delightful company. It is a shame, *monsieur*. But you must not despair!" he trilled.

Caroline looked up in surprise.

"I have no intention of despairing, *monsieur*. On the contrary, without these daily interruptions, I expect to accomplish a great deal!"

"Perhaps, my dear young man, perhaps. But it is not right that you should spend all your time in here." He spread his hands in a typical Gallic gesture, and Caroline smiled as he seemed to consider the matter.

"I have it!" he announced. "Tonight you will accompany me to Grillon's for dinner and then join me in my box at the theater."

"Oh, no, *monsieur*," cried Caroline, horrified at such a scheme. "I could not impose—"

"Nonsense! It will bring me great pleasure. It is settled, then; I will meet you at Grillon's at eight. *À bientôt,* Monsieur Pennington. Until this evening." The wiry man slipped through the door, totally ignoring Caroline's vehement protestations.

She was left standing with her mouth open, in midsentence. She slumped down into the chair as if in a trance, picked up her neglected teacup, and sipped the cold liquid.

What would the viscount say? Not only would

she be going against his wishes by appearing in society as Charles Pennington, but with the comte d'Épernon! On the other hand, she could not afford to get on the bad side of the comte, who appeared to know everyone of importance at White's.

After much thought, she decided to go. After all, she rationalized, an evening at Grillon's and the theater would be a new experience. And surely, she reasoned, such a sedate evening could not be objectionable?

Chapter Four

Caroline brushed Olivia's protests aside, not wanting to miss the tame adventure this night offered her. She dressed with care in buff-colored knee breeches and donned the dark brown velvet coat that fitted her rather more loosely than fashion dictated. Her snowy neckcloth was tied in a simple manner that managed to mask her bustline admirably. A narrow brown velvet ribbon held her brunette curls in place. Caroline struck a pose for Olivia, who pursed her lips and tut-tutted at her pupil.

"Come now, Aunt," coaxed Caroline, using her full-bodied "Mr. Pennington" voice. "Tell me how I look. Will I do?"

Olivia's laugh broke forth despite her worried frown. "Oh, you'll do, Caroline. But for what?"

"But, Livie, you know—"

"Yes, I know. But you remember this, now. Don't drink, and you won't lose your good judgment. I just have this awful feeling, Caroline."

"What? Woman's intuition?" she teased.

"Laugh if you will, but keep your wits about you, Caroline. I've never met this Comte d'Épernon, but I don't like him. What forty-five-year-old comte asks a young, impoverished clerk to dine with him and to share his box at the theater? I just want to remind you to be careful." The worried frown had reappeared, and Caroline hastened to reassure her. Then she picked up her walking stick and almost bolted for the door.

She stopped, one hand on the knob.

"Olivia? What about you? I'm afraid I'm being very inconsiderate. What will you do all evening?"

"I shall light a candle in the window and sit by the fire . . ." she intoned wanly, lifting a limp hand to her forehead.

"I have a little difficulty picturing that!" Caroline laughed. Then she added seriously, "But truly, Livie, are you tired of being here alone? Except for accompanying you to church on Sunday, I'm so rarely at home. I could stay; I don't have to leave."

"Good heavens, child! I have spent very little time in this house since we arrived in London. Don't be silly! I've been to shops and museums and art galleries. I daresay I've seen more of the city than you."

Caroline looked surprised.

"Remember, I'm a 'widow' and may do as I please, my dear. Why, only today I purchased this scarf on which you have failed to compliment me."

Caroline touched the paisley scarf and commented dutifully, "It is pretty, Livie; the swirling bright colors are very becoming on you."

Olivia's tone became brisk. "Now run along, do. I don't need your company every night; I can survive. Just you be careful, my dear young man!"

The entertainment began at Grillon's. Much to Caroline's surprise, the comte d'Épernon proved to be quite witty, and though relaxed, he managed to charm his young guest.

"Do you enjoy your work at our little club, *monsieur*?"

"Indeed I do, *monsieur le comte*. I find it very rewarding — even exciting," said Caroline enthusiastically.

The comte smiled. "I have been wondering, my young friend, how you come to have such a command of my language. Was your mother French, perhaps?"

"No, *monsieur le comte*, but my father was a professor of languages and literature at Cambridge. He took great pride in his ability to speak French and Italian, as well as Greek and Latin. To him, Latin was not a dead language."

"And you inherited this talent."

Caroline shook her head. "I only speak French. Of Greek and Latin, I can boast no extraordinary knowledge, except reading."

"You are too modest," he said, as the waiter appeared, flanked by two footmen bearing heavy silver trays.

"I hope you will enjoy your meal, Monsieur Pennington. Grillon's is famous for its food. Ah! Dinner!"

The first course consisted of relishes with curried crab dip, an excellent pheasant in Madeira, and a salad Niçoise. Each dish was prepared to perfection.

"Garçon," said Épernon, and the waiter appeared instantly. "My friend and I require champagne. Your best, of course."

Caroline's protests were waved aside, and she was soon watching the waiter pour the sparkling golden liquid into her glass. Champagne! she thought. I haven't allowed myself champagne since Papa gave me a glass on my eighteenth birthday. How giddy I was! And now I must drink it like a man. And I promised the viscount.

But the comte d'Épernon was waiting, his glass held in readiness for the toast. Caroline picked up her glass slowly and held her breath as the crystal goblets touched.

"To our young but growing friendship," said the comte solemnly.

Caroline contented herself with a nod and a small sip. Its coolness bubbled down her throat, which had suddenly gone dry. Another sip, then

Livie's warning came back to her and she resolutely set the glass on the table.

The waiter presented the next course, which boasted roast leg of lamb in paste with side dishes of minted glazed carrots, buttered peas with pearl onions, and roast duckling.

"Where did you live in France, *monsieur le comte*?" she inquired.

"At Épernon. It is about sixty kilometers from Paris. I have a *château* there. And, of course, a house in Paris."

Caroline was curious at his use of the present tense. "And you lost everything?"

The comte answered smoothly, *"Oui, mon ami*. But temporarily, only temporarily. Have you been to Paris, Monsieur Pennington?"

"No, though, of course, I hope to see it when things are better in France."

"Yes, you must. You will love France—the countryside, the cathedrals, and, of course, Paris. Yes, when my beloved country is one once more, you must go." The comte's voice held a curious mixture of longing and desperation. He looked up into Caroline's careful scrutiny and became jovial once again.

Refilling his own glass and adding to hers, he said, "Champagne, as I'm certain you know, is called after the region where it was first produced. But at Épernon, we produce a sparkling wine also. You will taste it with me one day, eh? We will spend just such an evening as this in my *château* at Épernon. We will take much time enjoying our little test."

"I accept your invitation, *monsieur le comte*, with pleasure," said Caroline, knowing this would never come to pass. It was a harmless comment to help the comte regain his good spirits.

She continued to allow small quantities of the potent wine to trickle down her throat. But as the meal wore on, she found it impossible to keep track of the amount, and the efficient waiter kept her glass filled to the brim at all times. Several times she began to lift it to her lips, moistened them, then returned the glass to the table.

"An excellent repast, *n'est-ce pas, mon ami?*" said the comte as they exited from Grillon's.

"Yes, it was wonderful, *monsieur*. Thank you." Caroline listened to her own words as she spoke. Perfectly enunciated, she concluded. Obviously the drink had little or no effect upon her this time.

"And now for our entertainment, eh?"

"I'm certainly looking forward to seeing Mrs. Siddons," said Caroline, leaning forward.

"Did you not hear, *cher* Pennington? The performance has been canceled for tonight. A small fire or something backstage. We will go some other time."

"Of course," agreed Caroline, but a sense of foreboding seized her, and she searched for some way to escape from the comte without offending him.

"I did not think you would greatly mind, my young friend," said the comte. "When one is young, a play is but a dull offering in a city such as London. *Moi,* I know this. Therefore, I have arranged for us to attend a most exclusive club."

"A club?" Caroline echoed.

"There will be faro and macao. And a most delightful hostess, I assure you. She and I . . ." He paused for effect and winked broadly. "We are very close, very close, indeed."

"How . . . convenient."

It was not the volume of Armand Pichette's laughter that planted the seed of panic in Caroline's breast, but the animalistic quality of it.

"Convenient? Yes, my friend, most convenient. And because you are the friend of the Comte d'Épernon, she has arranged a most special *rendezvous* for you."

"Rendezvous?" queried Caroline weakly.

"I have not met the young lady, but I have seen her. A delight to behold . . ."

Caroline froze in midstride, remaining perfectly still, her mind not yet able to digest this new dilemma.

"Monsieur Pennington, what is the matter?"

"I . . . I have just remembered."

The comte waited.

"I cannot stay gone so long."

"But, my dear Pennington, these things need not take so very long," countered Épernon with a wink.

"Nevertheless, I must return home now. It is imperative. My aunt . . ." Caroline shook the comte's hand with great force. "Thank you so much, *monsieur le comte,* for a most enjoyable evening."

"A pleasure, *mon vieux. Au revoir.*"

Caroline hurried down the street, hailed a hackney cab, and only relaxed her tense shoulders after collapsing against the uncomfortable squabs. She allowed herself a tremulous smile. Though she determined not to indulge in another such evening out on the town, she felt she had brushed through the ordeal fairly well.

If she had been privy to the Comte d'Épernon's expression as he watched her departure, she would have been less sanguine about her newest friend. His eyes narrowed to mere slits in his gaunt face, and his mouth twisted into a cruel smile.

"*Une autre fois, mon ami.* Another time, my very young friend," he murmured to the damp night air.

Ensconced in her favorite refuge early the next morning, Caroline indulged in the daydreams that had already cost her a night's sleep. There was nothing the comte had said that should cause her such unrest. An invitation to a club was not unusual, she knew. But still, there was some elusive element in the comte's conversation that unnerved her.

Considering her lack of sleep, it was not surprising that her deep contemplation in the quiet solitude of White's library should cause her to fall into a fitful slumber. It was still quite early when the door opened and the slight figure of the comte slipped inside.

He uttered not a word but stood watching

Caroline as she slept in the overstuffed armchair. A ray of sunshine fell on her face, giving her a very youthful, soft appearance. Just as before, the comte's eyes narrowed, and his expression was calculating and merciless.

"I've brought yer tea, Mr. Pennington," said Boggs, his voice causing Caroline to leap to her feet. "I knew ye'd be needing it, lad."

Boggs suddenly seemed to notice the comte.

"Excuse me, Mr. Pichette," he said (for he never deigned to call the *émigrés* by their titles). "I didn't see ye there. I suppose ye'll be wanting another cup?"

"No, you fool," he snapped as he turned to Caroline. "I thought to have a word with you, *mon ami,* but I can come back."

Rubbing her eyes, Caroline realized to what disadvantage she must appear and she nodded. The comte bowed and slipped away.

Boggs, who had maneuvered himself between the comte and his young charge, filled a cup with the strong brew. He handed it to the sleepy-eyed Caroline and appeared to reach the conclusion that he had best warn Mr. Pennington about his new friend.

"Harumph."

"Yes?" said Caroline in a gravelly voice.

"Beggin' yer pardon, sir, I'm sure."

"What is it, Boggs?"

"May I say a word or two about that comte fellow?"

Caroline bristled defensively.

"I don't see what business it is of yours, Boggs."

"I'm only following Lord Rosemeade's orders, sir."

Caroline's brown eyes sparkled, but she replied, "I assure you, Boggs, I am well able to take care of myself. And truly, I am so occupied here, I have little time to get into trouble."

"I beg yer pardon, Mr. Pennington, and I'll say only one other thing. Ye'd best ask yerself why was this Frenchie fellow standin' in 'ere a full minute while ye slept. That's all."

Boggs's question haunted Caroline throughout the day. Her work was slow and methodical, and she would sometimes find herself staring into thin air, realizing she had not moved for several minutes.

Boggs didn't trust the comte. Neither did the viscount. Why? Perhaps they just didn't like the French. In this time of unrest in France, many Englishmen looked down on and feared their neighbors from across the Channel.

And the comte had befriended her. He felt comfortable with her, able to speak freely in his native tongue. Not many of the club members had taken the time. She couldn't visualize the suave comte d'Épernon dragging her to some gambling hell by force, and she had managed to avoid last night's debacle. And she hated feeling confined by the prejudices of others, especially when she had so few acquaintances in London.

Why accept the viscount's opinion? Surely she

was mature enough to form her own. These would be as valid as his, she concluded.

Realizing how fruitless her day had been, Caroline decided to leave the club early in the afternoon. Forgoing a hackney cab on such a fine day, she chose a leisurely walk. She strolled down St. James's Street and into Bond Street, gazing into any window that caught her eye.

She was not truly paying attention to what she was doing when a voice at her elbow startled her.

"Ah, my young friend, you are interested in Madame Celeste's creations? A bit overstated, don't you think?"

"How do you do, *monsieur le comte*. Yes, but the work itself is quite good," said Caroline, recovering from being caught staring into the fashionable modiste's window. "My aunt, you know."

"I had forgotten you have an aunt with you in London. You must introduce me, Monsieur Pennington."

"Sometime I shall," she said out loud.

"You left early today, *mon ami*. I had hoped to speak with you."

"Yes?" she asked, strolling along with the elegant comte at her side.

"I am beside myself with joy," the comte began with growing excitement. "An old friend has escaped the Terror and has come to London. I saw him only this morning. I would like for you to meet him tomorrow evening at my home."

Taken unawares, Caroline answered, "I . . . I have an engagement . . . with my aunt."

Glancing sideways, she watched the comte's

face fall. Truly, she mused, he is so like a child with his highs and lows.

"I am so sorry to hear it, Monsieur Pennington. Gustave Thibault is a rare friend. He has even managed to bring with him two bottles of my sparkling wine from Épernon. I had hoped . . ." He grew silent.

Caroline stopped, reconsidering. Though unsure of the wisdom of it, she said, "Very well, *monsieur le comte*, my aunt will not mind waiting for one more day."

"How wonderful!" exclaimed the comte. "I will expect you at eight! *Au revoir.*"

He strode purposefully down the street and was soon lost in the crowd. Caroline continued on, oblivious to her surroundings, preoccupied not with the comte precisely, but with her employer, Robert Wyndridge, Viscount Rosemeade. She hoped he didn't learn of her dining with the comte. Rosemeade was not a man to cross.

"I should think you would avoid this comte after what happened the other night," said Olivia, her hands on her hips and her brow crinkled by a frown. She tried once again to dissuade Caroline from going.

"Oh, Livie, truly, I think I made too much of that situation. I was shocked, of course, and I panicked. It won't happen again."

"And when he throws some new situation your way?"

Caroline laughed, and Olivia realized it had been ages since she had heard Caroline's laugh sound so carefree. This masquerade seemed to be bringing her back to her old self despite the danger. Or, thought Olivia wisely, because of the element of danger. She smiled in spite of her deep concern.

"If I promise to be cautious, Mother Livie," Caroline said in a little girl's voice, "will you let me go out and play?"

"You will do as you please, as I well know, so I may as well give my blessing. But keep your wits about you, my dear, and be careful!"

"I will, Aunt!" promised Caroline, dropping a quick kiss on Livie's cheek before escaping out the door.

Olivia Stanton's expression grew severe again, and she whispered, "Do be careful, love."

"Mr. Pennington, m'lord," intoned the very proper butler, admitting Caroline to the comte's drawing room.

"Pennington, I was afraid you were not coming!"

"Please pardon my tardiness, *monsieur,* but my aunt and I were engaged in a discussion."

"Eh bien, you are here now; that is what matters. I would have you meet my old friend Gustave Thibault. Gustave, this is my charming new friend, Monsieur Charles Pennington."

"Bonjour," said Caroline politely. Her hand was taken and given one crushing shake, then released.

"Bonjour," replied Thibault, his voice gruff and loud, matching his hulking frame.

"I am so glad you two have met," said the comte. "Gustave speaks very little English, you see, and I thought your company would do much to ease his anxiety in a foreign land. You will not mind if we speak French, will you?"

"Certainly not," Caroline answered in perfect French, and they continued in this fashion.

"Gustave feared that all Englishmen were barbarians, unable and unwilling to learn our language. You are proof, my friend, that this is not so. Is that not true, Gustave?" asked the comte.

"Yes," growled Thibault, running his thick finger inside his cravat uncomfortably. Caroline wondered secretly if Thibault could speak any language at all, he was so silent.

The meal was a succession of one gourmet dish after another. The first course was led with a salmon mousse with cucumber dressing, followed by creamed mushrooms and chestnuts, a soufflé, and asparagus and artichokes. The creamy sauces left Caroline wishing for some plain English fare.

The comte guided the conversation, eliciting comments from Caroline and an occasional grunt from Thibault. Otherwise, the hulking Frenchman remained silent and sullen, watching Épernon and gulping one bite after another.

Chicken Richelieu with spiced apple rings and escalope de veau à la Normandie followed the first course. Caroline stifled a groan.

Two hours later, as the covers were cleared, the three gentlemen were left with a platter of fruits and cheeses and the bottle of wine.

The comte stood up, uncorking the precious liquid himself and then serving it with flair.

Trying to make conversation, Caroline asked Thibault, "How did you manage to secure two bottles of the comte's sparkling wine, *monsieur?*"

Thibault looked uncomfortable, and Épernon stepped in.

"A miracle, my young friend! Truly, there is no other way to describe it."

Caroline took a tentative sip. Searching for an adequate phrase that would please the comte, she said grandly, "A masterpiece, *monsieur,* a veritable masterpiece!"

Genuine pleasure lighted the comte's face as he watched her drink once again, and he thanked her effusively. Even Thibault was moved to smile (or at least Caroline assumed it was a smile).

The big man put the glass to his lips and said, "As always, marvelous, monseigneur."

Caroline's head snapped up at the title, and she intercepted the furious glare the comte shot Thibault. Thibault looked contrite and frightened.

She glanced away hastily, but not in time. The comte's quick weasel eyes had noticed her puzzled frown and they grew narrow and dangerous.

"I'm afraid, my friend, that it is time for our little charade to end," said the comte quietly.

"Charade?" she echoed. Every muscle tense, she was ready to spring for the door.

"Bien sûr, of course. Gustave," he commanded softly.

The one word brought the large man to his

feet instantly, and with a snakelike move, he grabbed Caroline, pinning her arms behind her with one hand. She started to scream, and with his other hand, he thrust a napkin into her mouth.

Struggle was useless. She grew still, and Thibault pushed her back into her chair. The comte smiled, his eyes no more than slits.

"A toast, Gustave, to our very young friend!"

Gustave gave a low chuckle and downed the entire contents of the glass. Then he pulled out a long cord and proceeded to lash Caroline to the chair.

Gustave and the comte held a whispered conference on one side of the room. The big man nodded and went out the door. The comte sat down beside the bottle of wine and consumed half of its contents in silence.

The house grew silent. An ormolu clock on the mantel chimed the hour: eleven o'clock.

Caroline's misery increased with each passing moment. She wondered how the comte had guessed her secret. She tried desperately to refrain from considering why he had ordered the attack on her. Her mental state was balanced precariously on the edge of panic each time a possible motive occurred to her. Olivia's words haunted her: "Be careful, be careful, be careful. . . ."

Just after midnight, noises came to her ears, signaling the return of Gustave Thibault. He entered, handed something to Épernon, and withdrew.

Placing the item in his large coat pocket, the comte rose and walked to her side. Leaning against the table, he looked at her for a full minute before speaking.

"I will remove the napkin, my dear. It would be useless to scream; there is no one to hear. Do you understand?"

Caroline nodded, and he wrenched the gag from her mouth. He extended the still-full glass of wine. She wanted to refuse but was too thirsty. She drained it as he put it to her lips.

"You are aware that I have discovered your little secret, eh?"

She stared ahead mutely.

"Yes, it was not difficult, *mademoiselle*. I was only curious at first, but a question or two in Cambridge and I knew all."

Caroline could not prevent her worry from showing.

"A poor plan, my dear, a very poor plan. But then, you thought to have only Englishmen to fool. Not such an arduous task as it is to fool a Frenchman."

He stretched out his hand and stroked her cheek with long, bony fingers. Quickly, she turned her head and bit his thumb.

He jerked back. Cursing, he nursed his hand for a moment; his black eyes blazed with anger. Then a cruel smile formed on his thin lips. Deliberately, he struck her on the side of the head. Caroline cried out in pain, her ears ringing, her temple pounding.

The comte walked back to his place and refilled the crystal goblet. His expression was pleasant while he watched the tears roll down her cheeks.

Caroline regained control as the pain lessened to a dull throb. The comte returned to her side, towering above her.

"Now, *mademoiselle,* we will talk." Caroline shot him a venomous look, but he seemed not to notice.

"As you have guessed, I have some plan in mind. You asked me once if I had lost everything in the Terror. I was not quite truthful with you then. It is true that I am exiled to England, but only because it is necessary to my mission. As an *émigré,* a wealthy one, I have access to many circles, like White's, where I may learn much information useful to my emperor. Bonaparte is very generous to those who serve him well, and I expect to have my estates restored after all this is over, and perhaps even more land. With all these foolish noblemen fleeing France, many estates will be available to those who are useful to Napoleon."

"So you are a spy as well as a traitor."

He shrugged his shoulders. "That depends on which side you are on, *mademoiselle.* As for me, I am merely being practical."

"What have I to do with all this? I don't know anything about military matters."

"Ah! But you have access to so many influential men!" he explained. "You have become—how do you say it?—a fixture at White's, where men—men important in government and military—go and relax. While relaxing, perhaps they drink more than is wise, and you are there to listen, to learn."

"They don't drink in the library," she said sarcastically.

"Ah, but when the door is open . . . Or when your eyes are tired, and you are feeling confined . . . *Alors,* one walks, one stretches, one hears."

"And?" she asked.

"And reports to me."

"No!" she exclaimed emphatically.

He pulled Olivia's gaily colored scarf from his coat pocket, saying deliberately, "Perhaps you will reconsider, eh?"

Chapter Five

Caroline had never before swooned. She awoke groggy, a headache pounding away, and tried to focus her eyes on the ceiling. The little clock struck the half hour, and she wondered how it could still be so early.

"So you are awake! How nice," said the comte.

She looked around, seeing his swarthy face and the colored scarf in a blur.

"It becomes late, my friend. We must make our plans so that you may return to Miss Stanton. We do not wish her to suspect."

"Then she isn't dead?" Caroline asked in disbelief.

"*Mon Dieu!* But you jump to conclusions so quickly. No, no, your Miss Stanton is quite safe at your cousin's town house. She is perhaps a little worried since you are out so late, but that is all."

"Then how . . . ?" she began, looking at the scarf.

"Ah, the scarf. Merely to show you that I can get into any place I wish, without anyone being made aware. A most useful talent in my business, I assure you."

Caroline shivered. "How will you stop me from going to the authorities?"

"I shan't. You may go, certainly, but I will know of it. Before they have had time to investigate, your Miss Stanton will be dead. Perhaps you, too, for that matter."

She still looked defiant, and he coaxed her.

"Come, now, *mademoiselle*. It is not so much I ask. You listen, you tell me anything that sounds promising, and I will decide from that point."

"And if I hear nothing?" she asked.

"But you will, *mademoiselle*, you will. Remember your aunt," he said, twisting the scarf around her neck in a calculating manner.

The next morning, Caroline dressed for White's with heavy eyes and a mind full of apprehension and impossible schemes. Once outside, she paused on the top step to flick some lint from her sleeve, then froze. Across the way, she spied the hulking figure of Gustave Thibault. He gave her his twisted smile in salute.

Caroline caught herself stepping back; then she squared her shoulders and walked down the stairs.

Every time she walked out to the main room that day, the comte was there. He greeted her warmly the first time. Afterward, he never looked up, but she could sense his awareness of her presence.

After tea, the door opened and the comte strode into the library and seated himself on the settee.

"Very good, Caroline, very good. Though perhaps you should not come out quite so often at first. They are not accustomed to that; it will take them a week or so. And your meals—begin taking your luncheon in the dining area."

"But would that not be thought strange, too?"

"Hmm, perhaps. I have it. Tomorrow, I will invite you to join me. That will be the beginning. From then on, you may say you need the air or something. You English are so dull, not inquisitive at all."

Caroline's heart was pounding like a trapped animal's. She said desperately. "Why don't you just do this? You can listen as easily as I!"

"I said the English are dull, not indiscreet. Though I am accepted here, they are not so open in my presence. But with a mere clerk? It will be different. A servant is invisible."

With this, the comte left. Caroline sat dumbfounded until she became aware of the clock chiming the hour. Eight o'clock. She realized with a start that it had grown quite dark; Livie would be worried.

She dragged herself out of the chair. Before she reached the door, Boggs entered.

"Mr. Pennington, I didn't know ye were still 'ere."

"I'm on my way out, Boggs," said Caroline.

Boggs watched her till she was out of sight, noting the listless gait and sagging shoulders. He went about snuffing the candles, muttering under his breath.

"Ain't right, the lad workin' all th' time. 'Tis makin' 'im weak and frail. Books . . . just books. A body's not meant to spend all 'is time sittin' over books."

"Is anything wrong, Caroline?" asked Livie later that evening as they took coffee in the drawing room after dinner. Caroline, too exhausted to change, had remained in her breeches and coat. Livie's tatting shuttle lay motionless in her lap as she watched the younger woman.

Caroline smiled at the query, saying, "Only that I am fagged to death, Aunt, but I'm too engrossed in this volume to leave it right now."

"Is that why you've turned only one page this past hour?" asked Livie.

"Indeed," replied Caroline. "I'm afraid my Latin is inadequate for much of this. I should have paid more attention to Papa!" She met Livie's eyes, managing an air of self-mockery calculated to put her mentor's mind at rest.

Though Miss Stanton was not deceived, she judged it improbable that Caroline would unburden herself that evening. She yawned prettily and put aside the trail of fine lace she had been working on.

"I fear I cannot see well enough to continue. I'll just say good night."

"Good night, Livie. Sleep well," Caroline said with a feeling of relief.

Pausing at the door, Livie asked, "Caroline, I wondered if you'd seen my new shawl?"

"New shawl?" she echoed.

"Yes, the paisley scarf I just purchased," Olivia explained, puzzled by the flash of emotion in Caroline's eyes. What had it been? Certainly not surprise. What, then? Fear?

"No, Livie, I've not seen it," Caroline answered in a strong voice. "Have you lost it?"

"Misplaced it. No doubt it will turn up. Good night, dear."

"Good night."

Caroline closed her book as the door clicked shut. She stretched her aching arms and stood up, reaching skyward to ease her tense muscles. She walked to the window, cautiously pulling the heavy curtains aside until she could peep out. Peering into the gloom, she looked toward the street lamp and breathed a deep sigh of relief. No sign of Thibault!

But even as she formed this happy thought, a figure stepped out of the shadow of the house; the man's face was turned up, lit by the glow of his cigar. She gasped, and twitched the curtain back into place.

Fairly running to the door of the drawing room, she forced her actions to evince a calm she could not feel. This was fortunate, for Bates was in the main hall, making certain the front door was secure for the night.

She nodded. "Good night, Bates."

"Good night, miss."

Once in her chamber, she turned the key and hurried to each window, checking the locks. Satisfied that she was as secure as possible for the moment, Caroline began to strip off her clothes, ridding herself of all vestiges of Mr. Pennington. She poured tepid water into the china basin and, wetting a cloth, began to scrub herself from head to toe. The shock of the cool water and her vigorous scouring left her skin red and tingling.

She donned the beribboned nightgown and crawled into bed, to lie awake in comfort and to castigate herself for a fool.

And yet Caroline recognized that the comte would have created his own opportunity to enlist her in his nefarious activities. But she still could not believe she had been so obliging, so very gullible.

If only the viscount were in town, she thought, then uttered a prayer of thanksgiving that he was not. He could not help her out of her difficulty. And she felt certain she could not have concealed anything from those probing gray eyes. No, she would have to find her own solution to this dilemma. In the meantime, she would make certain any information she passed along was completely useless to the comte.

"The coq au vin is passable, my friend, but I wouldn't advise the vichysoisse," said the Comte d'Épernon casually as he and Caroline seated themselves in the club's dining room. Caroline failed to respond, and his weasel eyes narrowed.

"You must appear to be enjoying my company, *mon ami*," he hissed quietly.

She glanced at his face and looked away quickly, but she knew he required an answer. "I find both dishes quite tasty, *monsieur le comte*," she commented perversely.

"As you will, Charles," he said, stressing the name.

So, she must continue to employ the comte's given name? She seethed. Well, she would just see about that!

"Have you heard from Rosemeade?" he asked.

"No, but I hadn't expected to do so."

"He will no doubt be returning soon," said the comte. "He will not miss Lady Lietchfield's masked ball."

"Lady Lietchfield?" asked Caroline, concentrating fiercely on her soup.

She missed the amused gleam in the comte's dark eyes.

"Augusta, Lady Lietchfield; she has recently emerged from mourning," he explained helpfully, the malicious light growing more noticeable.

"Mourning?" echoed Caroline.

"Her husband, Baron Lietchfield, was killed near the Rhône almost two years ago." He lowered his voice to a mere whisper as he added, "Very convenient for your viscount, *mademoiselle*."

Caroline's head jerked up, and she realized he was making game of her. Her brown eyes flashed as she searched for a devastating rejoinder.

But the comte continued tormenting her, saying, "I quite understand your infatuation with that gentleman. A *physique magnifique!*"

"*Tais-toi, âne*," she whispered in return with a smile.

The comte threw back his head, laughing out loud, causing a number of the members to turn momentarily.

"Insults, my dear Charles, are not your forte. Being called an ass is not likely to bruise my ego."

I should like to bruise something else, thought Caroline.

Then the comte rose, his attitude brisk, and announced, "We are finished. You must show me that book you were telling me about, Charles."

Once they had reached the solitude of the library, Épernon was all business. "What news today?"

"I'm afraid there is almost nothing."

The comte regarded her for a moment, his dark head tilted to one side. His voice, when he finally spoke, was so low, Caroline had to strain to hear his words.

"It is well, young Pennington, that you are

afraid to have 'almost nothing' to report. I can employ methods that will make you pray to have information for me."

She shivered but did not alter her stance or drop her gaze.

"I still have very little for you, *monsieur le comte,*" Caroline said with only a slight quiver in her voice.

Épernon stretched out his long arm, taking her upthrust chin in his bony fingers. He pulled her face close to his, staring relentlessly into her eyes. Bile rose in her throat and she swallowed hard.

He laughed and pushed her back. Caroline caught herself on the table before she hit the floor, the fear that gripped her plain on her face.

"Now, tell me what you have heard," the comte commanded.

Caroline crawled onto the settee and complied. "Sir Lionel mentioned that his son has been ordered to return to his unit."

"Hardly useful, my friend. One wounded officer returning to his unit?"

"A unit that has been ordered to sail in two weeks' time," she added, hoping he wouldn't learn of the small lie. Sir Lionel had actually said one week.

The comte's relaxed figure tensed. "To sail where?" he demanded.

"I've no idea," she replied.

"And what else?"

"Nothing!"

"Nothing, my friend?"

Caroline hesitated before answering. "There was a man—I didn't recognize him—who was saying the Home Office is in a state. A shipment of uniforms is missing, and they are desperately needed in Spain before the end of June." Again she distorted the information; the day mentioned had been the end of May.

"Now, that is quite interesting," murmured Épernon.

Caroline wanted to question him but could not bring herself to ask how he might utilize such information. Better not to know, she decided miserably.

Days later, she wished she had asked the comte, for she heard more about the shipment of uniforms. Unsure just how damaging this information could prove, she felt she must remain silent. But, unfortunately, this was the only tidbit of news she had overheard that day, and she dreaded the comte's arrival.

He would be suspicious if she reported nothing. Though she could deny having had time to enter the main rooms, she didn't dare. She had tried this gambit only two days before, and the comte had expressed patent disbelief. She had ended by telling him the one piece of information she had intercepted. As a result, she was wary of lying to him about her activities. Caroline felt certain he had other spies at White's.

Caroline passed the entire afternoon absorbed in her problem. She simply could not lose herself in the books as she had before. Trying to divert herself, she picked up a dog-eared copy of *Tristram Shandy*. Thumbing through it, she noted that someone had underlined the more shocking passages, but she could not concentrate even on this. In disgust, she pitched it onto a tall stack of books, causing it to topple over.

As she bent down to gather the books, Caroline failed to hear the door open. Her posture was not a flattering one, and Viscount Rosemeade chuckled to find his employee upended.

"Still up to your, uh, ears in books, I see," he drawled lazily.

Caroline skyrocketed to her feet, her face crimson. "My lord!" she exclaimed. "You startled me!"

His lordship regarded her with curiosity. The thought flashed through his mind once again that any maiden would envy Miss Pennington her ability to blush so becomingly. He wondered how she would appear properly gowned.

"Sorry, Pennington. I just thought I'd step in to see how you are faring."

Feeling suddenly defensive, she snapped, "You needn't check up on me, my lord. I would never shirk my responsibility just because you've absented yourself from town."

The viscount's wicked brow arched, and his gray eyes glowered with disdain. Caroline shifted from one foot to the other, biting her lip in anticipation of Rosemeade's biting scold. Instead, his tone was surprisingly sympathetic.

"Been having a time of it?"

She raised her eyes to meet his, resisting an absurd desire to throw herself on his breast and collapse into tears. To be comforted by those strong arms! To be able to give all her problems over to his broad shoulders! She felt, somehow, the ghosts and goblins would magically disappear in his capable hands. However, none of these outrageous thoughts could be read on her penitent countenance.

"It has been hectic, my lord, but I had no right to rip at you so. My apologies."

Lord Rosemeade sensed that this statement did not reflect Miss Pennington's precise thoughts, but he forbore to press her. He waved his hand as though this mere physical movement could blot out the unpleasant words.

Taking his cue, Caroline inquired, "And how was your journey, my lord?"

"Excellent. Mr. Farningham is convinced that introducing this new bloodline into my stable will return us to the winner's circle."

"You must be very well pleased."

"Yes," he said thoughtfully, "though it will never be a matter of grave import to me. It is merely an amusement."

"Like your books, my lord?" asked Caroline.

"No, though Ferdie would be scandalized to hear me say so. Books have always provided me more pleasure than horses."

"Amen to that!" said Caroline fervently.

The viscount's great laugh sounded strangely

in the somber room. Caroline joined in but was silenced by Rosemeade's next comment.

"Henry tells me you've not ridden since I left. We must remedy that. Tomorrow at ten?"

Caroline allowed her gaze to travel significantly from the books stacked on the floor to those on the table to the one she held in her hands.

"I really shouldn't abandon my efforts now, my lord, even for a morning."

The viscount cocked his head to one side, a smile threatening to break forth. He spoke quietly, his tone caressing her ears. "You are probably the only young lady in London who would decline to ride with Viscount Rosemeade. I do believe I am shocked," he concluded piously.

Caroline was not fooled; her brown eyes danced as she responded gallantly, "There is no need for you to feel downcast, my lord, I assure you. It is not your company I disdain, but the manner in which we progress as we converse."

"Ha! Well said!"

A puzzling chit, thought the viscount. She's so complacent about her awkward situation, not batting an eye as she turns down my rather condescending invitations.

"What do you do at night, Miss Pennington?" he inquired.

"Why, I . . . I go home, have dinner, relax," replied Caroline, wondering both at the question and at his laxness in addressing her as Miss. It seemed out of character, somehow.

"Do you and your charming aunt never go out?"

"We haven't had any opportunity yet. Though, of course, I dined at your house. Oh, and at Grillon's one evening," she added, hoping to make her life sound a little less mundane.

"At Grillon's?" echoed Rosemeade. "And how did Mrs. Stanton like our little hotel?"

Caught in her own trap!

"She . . . that is, I didn't go with my aunt."

"Oh?"

Goaded by his supercilious attitude, she confessed hurriedly, "I was the comte's guest."

The viscount's gaze narrowed. She expected him to rebuke her, but he held himself in check.

"I hope you enjoyed yourself," he commented blandly.

Defensive again, she squared her jaw and said, "It was delightful."

"How nice. But I digress. If you feel you cannot leave your work just now, then I will not press you. Good day."

Caroline had to restrain herself from reaching out to him.

"Good-bye, my lord," she murmured, her misery wrapping around her like a heavy winter cloak.

The viscount stopped outside the library and leaned against the door, his expression thoughtful. Boggs entered the corridor.

"Hello, Boggs," the viscount said, and began to walk away.

"M'lord?" Boggs hesitated. "M'lord, I'm not wishful of interfering, but being one who keeps 'is eyes open, I can't 'elp but see things."

"Cut line, Boggs. Out with it," said Rosemeade impatiently.

"Well, sir, m'lord, the lad," he said, nodding toward the library, "is often in the company of that French fellow who calls 'isself a count." Boggs sniffed loudly as he pronounced the word *count*.

"Mr. Pennington told me they had dined together at Grillon's."

"And at 'is house, m'lord. And 'ere in the club."

Rosemeade's brow furrowed as he calculated the possible motive behind the comte's friendliness to a penniless clerk. He shook his head, unable to arrive at any satisfactory conclusions.

"What do you mean to do about it, m'lord? I hate to see Mr. Pennington in the clutches o' that Frenchie!"

The viscount placed a reassuring hand on the servant's shoulder. "I suppose," he uttered wearily, "I shall be forced to wean our young friend away from the evil Comte d'Épernon."

"Robert! How delightful to have you back! I have missed you," said Lady Lietchfield, holding out both hands to the viscount.

He planted a chaste kiss on the back of one hand before turning to the other occupant of the parlor.

The Scandalous Miss

"Good morning, Lady Hensley. I trust you are well."

"Tolerable, Robert. And you? Did you enjoy your little sojourn in the country?"

"Yes, ma'am, as much as a man can when he has only other men and horses for company."

"Very pretty, my lord," said the dowager with a laugh. "Now I shall leave you two young people. I have an appointment with Andre." She allowed the viscount to bow over her hand and then disappeared, closing the door. Augusta gave the viscount a rueful grin.

"You must pardon my mother, Robert. She wouldn't act so if you weren't so eligible. Andre won't be here to do our hair until this afternoon."

He chuckled and strode to the window; the bright sunlight filtered through the yellow draperies, making his chestnut hair glint with gold. Then he turned the topic. He and Lady Lietchfield had been friends since childhood, and their connection was certainly not romantic.

"Is all in readiness for tomorrow?"

"I believe so. Mama is in a tizzy, of course, but we wouldn't be entertaining without that. You must tell me what costume you've chosen, Robert."

"Costume? Now, Augusta, you know how I feel about masquerades. I've my black silk domino."

She made a moue. "Such a bore, Robert! You should come as Arthur or an Elizabethan pirate."

Robert changed the subject again. "Augusta, if I get up a house party to spend the month of July at Rosemeade, will you come? With your mother, of course."

She hesitated. He knew she disliked the country, but if he was asking, he must have a compelling reason.

Lowering her eyes, Augusta murmured, "Yes, Robert, I'll come."

"Excellent!" He beamed. "I'll invite Ferdie, perhaps Julian and Abbie, and—"

"Hardly good company for Mama, Robert," she put in.

"Hmm. True, Augusta, but I'll not have some dowager with a simpering daughter in tow bothering Ferdie. Not even for your mama."

She nodded, knowing he referred to her mother's bosom friend, Lady Oglethorpe, a delightful woman, but her daughter was a large, horse-faced damsel whose laugh matched her face. Though Ferdie loved the animals, he couldn't abide such a countenance on a female.

"I have it!" said the viscount artlessly. "Caroline Pennington and her aunt, Mrs. Stanton."

Augusta's brow wrinkled.

"I don't believe I am acquainted . . ."

"Of course not, but you shall meet them! Miss Pennington's brother is the young man I told you about; he's cataloguing the library at my club."

"A clerk?" she said. "Robert, I know how democratic you are, but really—"

"They're of a very good family, I assure you.

The aunt is the widow of Stanton," he added, hoping he had spoken the truth.

"Pennington," she said, savoring the name. "That sounds familiar."

"It should; their cousin is Pennington Wickersham."

"Penn Wickersham!" she exclaimed in disgust. "That fribble! That—"

"Now, Augusta, Charles Pennington is nothing like his cousin. He doesn't drink, doesn't gamble—that I am aware of—doesn't womanize. . . . Why, he doesn't even ride!"

Augusta turned laughing eyes on her companion.

"Then why on earth would you wish to invite him to Rosemeade for a month?"

"Actually, I don't intend to. He's too wrapped up in his work, though I think it would relieve his mind to know his aunt and sister are happy. He does worry over them. His aunt seems a delightful woman; I'm sure your mother would like her. And the sister is sensible. I tell you what, Augusta, let me take you to meet them this morning. And your mother, too."

Flattered that Robert was allowing her to choose his guests for the proposed house party, she agreed and ran upstairs to change and to apprise her mother of the outing.

"Show them in, Bates," said Olivia Stanton, silently thanking the stars that she had planned to go out and thus was dressed in her smart sea-green walking gown. She rose to greet her visitors.

"Mrs. Stanton, we are glad to find you at home," said the viscount, bowing over her hand. "Lady Hensley and her daughter, Lady Lietchfield, this is Mrs. Stanton."

Greetings traveled from one party to another. Seated at last, a desultory conversation developed.

"Caroline will be sorry she was not in; she is out shopping."

"We'll look forward to meeting her another time. Tell me, Mrs. Stanton, are you related to the Hereford Stantons?" asked Lady Hensley.

"As a matter of fact, I am," replied Olivia truthfully, causing the viscount to smile.

"You wouldn't be Sinclair Stanton's daughter-in-law, would you?" continued Lady Hensley, delving into this family ancestry with relish.

"No, my lady. His daughter."

Lady Hensley looked confused, and Olivia obliged her guest with an explanation.

"My husband was also a Stanton. A distant cousin, you know, from near Edinburgh." Olivia crossed her fingers in the folds of her gown as the lie rolled off her tongue.

"Ah." Her ladyship sighed, glad to have the connection clarified. "You have an older brother, don't you?"

"Yes, James."

"I remember James Stanton. Such a handsome young man he was! Where is he now?"

"He's at home. When Father turned sixty, he

told James the lands were his responsibility and retired to his library."

"A wise man," said Lady Hensley. "Mrs. Stanton, I realize this is short notice, and I hope you won't be offended, but we are having a ball tomorrow night, a masquerade ball. Won't you and your niece and nephew please come? It's likely to be a sad crush, but I would love for you to attend."

During this invitation, Augusta watched the viscount. His expression was smug. She wondered at his engineering this elaborate plan. She studied Mrs. Stanton; a handsome woman, perhaps a year or two older than the viscount. Odd, she concluded. Perhaps the niece was the attraction. She resolved to watch that situation carefully at the ball.

"I'm afraid my nephew does not go out in society, but my niece and I would be delighted, Lady Hensley. Thank you so much for including us." She turned to the viscount. "And thank you, Lord Rosemeade, for bringing Lady Hensley and Lady Lietchfield to call."

"My pleasure, Mrs. Stanton. Perhaps I can offer to stop by for you and Miss Pennington tomorrow?"

Olivia was not proud, but she was beginning to feel like a charity case. "That won't be necessary. We have Penn's carriage at our disposal. Thank you, my lord."

He nodded, gathered his two pigeons, and herded them out, well pleased with how things had evolved.

* * *

Unaware of the delights soon to come her way, Caroline worked on in the library. Expecting the comte at any moment, it took a great deal of self-discipline to remain in the quiet room.

The shadows had grown long on the walls when word finally came from the comte. Boggs delivered the brief message, which Caroline accepted with a trembling hand.

"From Mr. Pichette's man, sir."

"Thank you, Boggs." When the servant lingered, Caroline's taut nerves led her to snap, "That will be all, Boggs."

"Aye, sir," said Boggs as he ambled out the door.

Caroline ripped open the seal, but she was shaking so badly she couldn't read the words at first. After she forced herself to sit, she took a deep breath. Holding the missive in her lap, she read:

> *Charles, I must cancel our engagement for this evening. Business requires that I leave London for a few days. We will get together when I return.*
>
> *Armand*

Returning from White's later that evening, Caroline whistled as she tripped up the steps. Not even a sign of Thibault!

"Caroline, the most extraordinary thing happened this morning!" exclaimed Livie, bursting with her news as she followed Caroline into her room.

"What was that, Aunt?"

"We received an invitation to a masquerade ball. All the ton will be there!"

"Livie, are you dreaming? Who would invite us to a ball?"

"Well, I suspect it was your viscount's doing—"

"Hardly my viscount," protested Caroline.

"Nevertheless, he brought Lady Hensley and her daughter for a morning call, and the next thing I knew, I was accepting the invitation!"

"But, Livie, we don't even have the right type of clothes."

"Nonsense! I have sent Bates out to procure dominoes for us. We will be quite unexceptional."

"And our clothes underneath these dominoes. What will everyone think at the unmasking?"

"Heavens, child, you don't take your domino off! Only your mask. I tell you, Caroline, it quite takes me back!"

Caroline looked at her. Olivia Stanton never spoke of her life before becoming governess to Professor Pennington's motherless little girl. Caroline had always supposed Livie's life to have been one of genteel poverty.

"How does it take you back, Livie?" she asked, unable to contain her curiosity.

Livie blushed, embarrassed by her own enthusiasm. "I . . . I had a season once—or part of one, anyway."

"You, Livie? Why didn't you ever tell me?"

"It never seemed of any consequence. And it

was so very long ago. That young girl doesn't exist anymore."

"What happened?"

Olivia gave a sad smile. She sighed, then woke to Caroline's questioning brown eyes.

"I was so very foolish. One month into the Season, I ran away with a young man. We were married—illegally, of course—and we spent one blissful week together before my brother James found us. He took me home. Our parents had the marriage annulled, and I never saw him again."

"Annulled after a week as man and wife?"

"With wealth and power anything is possible. My father hated my husband's father so, he refused to accept the marriage. I was so full of romantic ideals. I expected my husband to ride *ventre à terre* to my rescue. When I finally realized he wasn't coming, I signed the agreement of the annulment."

"How . . . how awful," declared Caroline. She was the practical sort, but Livie's bittersweet smile tugged at her heart.

"What happened to him?"

"I've no idea. I've not seen him since. Two years later, my father finally consented to allow me to go to work for your father, and you have been my life ever since."

"Oh, Livie! I'm so sorry!" said Caroline, giving her friend an impulsive hug. Olivia Stanton brightened, shaking her head to disclaim any great tragedy.

"I haven't been pining, believe me. I doubt that my brief marriage would have remained blissful. My husband was horse-mad. That's all he ever cared about. So you see, Caroline, I have a week full of delightful memories and no regrets."

Silence reigned for a few moments.

Caroline mused, "So that's where you learned to tie a cravat."

Miss Stanton giggled.

"Not exactly. I learned then, but I kept in practice on your father. He made me swear not to tell, but that man couldn't tie a bow, much less his cravat! And since your papa was so eccentric as to refuse to hire a valet, he was glad to have my help."

"Papa? Well, of all things!"

"But, Caroline, back to tomorrow night. You will go with me, won't you?"

"I should be delighted, my lady," she said, and executed an elegant bow any tulip of the ton would have envied.

Chapter Six

The Hensley ballroom was a vision of canary yellow with curtains of Hanover blue. Yellow silk was draped from the ceiling medallion and attached to the tops of the walls. From each corner more yellow silk spilled carelessly onto the floor. Huge Chinese vases filled with roses stood along the walls.

Caroline stopped just inside the entrance and gazed raptly at this scene; the swirl of costumed dancers added to the dizzying effect.

"Well, Miss Pennington, what do you think?" asked a deep voice just above her shoulder.

"I see my domino and mask are ineffectual, my lord," she said, glancing over to see those gray eyes peering through the slits of a black mask.

"Not precisely. I had been watching for you and your aunt. It's not difficult to identify people in pairs. But you didn't answer: How do you like Lady Lietchfield's brainstorm?"

Caroline turned back to the ballroom hesitantly. She remained silent, not realizing her lip had curled slightly.

The viscount's booming laughter rang out clearly above the din. Eyes turned, wondering at the sight of Viscount Rosemeade—for that rich laugh could belong to none other—and his nervous female companion. Lady Lietchfield watched, too, from her station at the door.

Caroline looked up at him sheepishly. "I don't wish to be disrespectful, my lord, for I know you and Lady Lietchfield . . ." Under Rosemeade's sardonic regard, she lost track of her words.

"You were saying," he prompted. "Lady Lietchfield and I what?"

"I . . . that is, you are friends. And I am ignorant of such matters."

"Nevertheless, you have good taste, and your opinion is just as valid as anyone else's might be."

"Very well, my lord, it seems a bit much, don't you think?"

"You mean you are not inspired by this gloriously ostentatious profusion of silk? Why, the choice of colors makes me absolutely . . . bilious!"

Now it was Caroline's turn to be surprised, and she broke into laughter. The viscount, realizing their amusement was being remarked on, hooked arms with Miss Pennington and propelled her toward the refreshment tables.

There he introduced her to another young lady and her two male companions. Caroline looked away as the other young lady detached the viscount and led him to the dance floor.

When Caroline next encountered the viscount, she was entering the supper room and the viscount hailed her to join his party, neatly detaching her from her last dance partner. Augusta noted the brotherly camaraderie the viscount showed toward Miss Pennington. She determined to befriend the young lady.

Masks were removed upon entering the supper room; the air was filled with sounds of surprise and blushing explanations.

Augusta had dressed daringly as a young boy of twenty-five years before. Her costume consisted of knee breeches and a waistcoat of sky-blue satin, a snowy fall of lace at her throat, and a bright yellow satin coat. The colors perfectly duplicated those of the ballroom as well as the lady's eyes and golden hair.

Without the mask to hide the viscount's scrutiny, Caroline found herself struggling to greet her hostess with a straight face. But Lady Lietchfield had set herself to charm the viscount's protégée and soon had Caroline at ease.

"Miss Pennington was telling me earlier how much she liked your decorations, Augusta. She only wished she'd chosen a different color of domino. The rose color clashes."

"Robert, don't tease Miss Pennington," said Augusta, turning kind eyes on the newcomer. "Don't pay any attention to his lordship, Miss Pennington; he's a sad rattle."

"I promise I shan't let his comment weigh me down, my lady," responded Caroline, hoping she was carrying on as a young lady of the ton would. She was painfully aware of the viscount's penetrating eyes and of his arm resting on Lady Lietchfield's chair. But Lady Lietchfield was speaking, and though Caroline was prepared to dislike the lady, she knew she must be polite.

"Your aunt and my mother seem to be cultivating their new friendship," commented Lady Lietchfield, nodding toward a nearby table where Lady Hensley and Olivia were seated with two other chaperones.

"I want to thank you for inviting us, Lady Lietchfield. I fear my aunt is rather lonely; she has not many friends in town."

"We were happy to oblige, of course, but you should really thank Lord Rosemeade. It was he who made a point of introducing us to your aunt."

Caroline turned and thanked the viscount self-consciously. Why had he done so? She could think of no motive except that he had been quicker than she to recognize the solitary social life Livie faced. He dismissed her words; Augusta breathed another sigh and relaxed.

"I understand your cousin is Penn Wickersham." Caroline nodded. "I had wondered where he came by such an unusual first name," commented Augusta.

"He was named for my father. Papa allowed Penn's parents to live with us when they married against their parent's wishes. Our mothers were sisters. All was forgiven eventually. Penn is the only paternal grandchild."

"I see," said Lady Lietchfield.

The viscount laughed and explained, "I'm afraid, Miss Pennington, Augusta does not get on with sporting gentlemen such as your cousin. As a matter of fact, she barely tolerates Ferdie."

"The only reason I do is because I am so seldom in his company. His only topic of conversation is horses, and I rarely frequent the stables." The words were haughty, but the twinkle in Lady Lietchfield's blue eyes removed their sting.

Caroline found herself liking Augusta. And Lady Lietchfield, with the specter of jealousy laid to rest, began to warm to her guest.

"Ah, here's Ferdie now!"

"My lady," said Ferdie Farningham with a negligent bow. "Robert."

"Hullo, Ferdie. May I present Miss Caroline Pennington."

Ferdie turned to greet Caroline with impatience before seating himself and addressing the viscount.

"Robert, by next spring you're going to have some of the most promising foals in the country," he enthused.

"I appreciate your overseeing the, uh, operations," answered Rosemeade with a quick glance toward Lady Lietchfield. She rolled her eyes in boredom, but Ferdie failed to notice. Caroline listened, not so much interested in the topic but in the display of such knowledge. Surely, she marveled, there was nothing about animal husbandry or bloodlines that Ferdie Farningham didn't know.

Lady Lietchfield finished her meal in silence. She was not petulant, only bored. When the music began again, and still Ferdie rattled on, she excused herself and fled.

The supper room was soon empty, save for a few. A scraping of chairs behind Caroline signaled to her that Olivia and Lady Hensley were following the rest and returning to the ballroom.

Caroline looked up, meaning to ask her aunt if

she was enjoying herself. Olivia's ashen face and rounded eyes arrested her. Ferdie Farningham had even paused in his dissertation, Caroline realized. It was Ferdie who broke the silence.

"Olivia?" he said quietly with a slight nod of his head.

"Ferdie," she replied, took a deep breath, smiled back at Lady Hensley, and proceeded on to the ballroom.

The viscount directed a questioning look at Caroline. She shrugged her shoulders, unable to shed any light on what had just passed.

"Ferdie," began the viscount, trying the direct approach. "How is it you know Miss Pennington's aunt?"

"Who? Oh, you mean Olivia," he said.

"Yes, Olivia Stanton."

"We, uh, knew each other many years ago," he answered, watching the doors to the other room.

"So, she never married," mused Ferdie.

"She's a widow, Mr. Farningham," supplied Caroline.

"Widow, eh?" He stood suddenly. "If you will excuse me, I believe the orchestra is beginning a waltz."

Lord Rosemeade regarded the diminutive figure of his old friend disappearing hastily into the crowd.

"Miss Pennington, since it is the waltz, and you've not been sanctioned to dance it yet, would you care to observe this phenomenon with me?" said the viscount.

"Phenomenon?" queried Caroline.

"Indeed, there is no other name for it when Ferdie Farningham leaves off discussing horseflesh in order to dance!"

Caroline laughed and took the viscount's arm to return to the ballroom, where couples whirled about on the hardwood floor. Many mothers still refused to allow their daughters to waltz, so the floor was not terribly crowded. They had little trouble discovering Olivia in the arms of Ferdie Farningham, nor was it difficult to discern the serious, almost melancholy expressions engraved on both of their countenances.

Caroline itched to get Olivia alone and question her, but the music seemed to go on forever. By the time the last chord sounded, Olivia was wearing her mask of serenity and Mr. Farningham was looking piqued.

Excusing herself to Rosemeade, Caroline crossed the short distance to Olivia, only to be met with a distracted "Let's go home."

Since Olivia was already turning to Lady Hensley and taking her leave, Caroline had no choice but to follow suit.

Once installed in Cousin Penn's carriage, Olivia shut her eyes, clutching her little gold-colored mask and beaded reticule, her shoulders and back straight and stiff.

Caroline pretended not to notice. "I am so glad you insisted I practice dancing with you, Aunt. I would have been in a quandary if you hadn't!" Pausing in vain for some response, Caroline continued. "Did you see that woman dressed as a page? I couldn't help but wonder how she ever got into those breeches. Of course, Lady Lietchfield was not much better; she only possessed a much better figure. What did you think of her? I must admit, I thought her quite nice. Though I—"

"Caroline, I have the most dreadful headache. Do you think we could ride home in silence?" Olivia Stanton pleaded.

"Certainly, Aunt. Not another word."

Next morning, Caroline was up early despite their late night. She had hoped to speak with her aunt, but Olivia was still asleep. Caroline had heard noises coming from Livie's room off and on until the sky was turning gray. Whatever memories the encounter with Ferdie Farningham had evoked, they were obviously not restful ones.

It was almost noon before Caroline reached the refuge of White's library. Forcing all issues from her mind, she progressed quite well until tea time.

This refreshment she took in the main lounge and was soon rewarded by the entrance of two young officers wearing scarlet regimentals. She strained to hear what passed between them and Lord Haversham, an official of the Home Office.

"Charles, *mon cher,* how are you? I hope you are not annoyed with me for missing our *rendezvous.*"

"Of course not, *monsieur,*" lied Caroline, her

blood congealing at the sound of Épernon's voice.

"Perhaps this evening, Charles?" asked the comte.

"I'm afraid not; I have plans," Caroline snapped.

"Plans that may be changed, eh?" the comte said sweetly, his countenance belying his tone.

Caroline trembled and acquiesced. It would do her no good to postpone the inevitable.

"Excellent, my friend! I will pick you up at eight, *oui*?" The comte rose and made his way to the door.

"Rosemeade! How charming to have you once again in our midst!" gushed the comte. "But then, I knew you would not miss a certain lady's ball, eh?"

"Épernon," acknowledged the viscount.

On hearing the exchange, Caroline made her way to the library. She needed a few moments before facing the viscount. She struck what she hoped was a thoughtful pose by the fireplace, a book in one hand. Recalling her first meeting with Lord Rosemeade, when she had waited like this, she smiled at her image in the mirror above the mantel.

The door opened, and Caroline was suddenly gazing into those steely gray eyes, now fraught with concern. Her heart melted at his kindness.

"Pennington, I want a word with you," he began as he closed the door.

"Yes, my lord?"

His crooked grin appeared, and he ran a hand through his chestnut-colored hair. "Could you sit down? I know I'd like to do so."

"Certainly. Now, what is it, my lord?"

Rosemeade shot the young woman a harried look. Forgetting caution, he asked, "Do you think, Miss Pennington, you could drop the 'my lords'? At least some of the time."

"Certainly, my . . . sir."

"Never mind. I will be direct, Miss Pennington. Is Épernon being a bother to you?"

"Bother?" she echoed, causing the viscount's face to take on an even more harassed aspect.

"Dammit, girl! Quit repeating everything I say," he snapped.

"But, my lord, I haven't been—"

"Forget it. Just answer me. If Épernon is making a nuisance of himself . . ."

"No, my lord," said Caroline. "He is not 'bothering' me. I don't particularly care for the comte, but one cannot be rude."

"Why not? I see no reason to be anything more than civil to someone like Épernon."

"But you and I are in different cases, my lord. The comte d'Épernon has expressed an interest in my work here," lied Caroline. As the viscount's brow rose skeptically, she elaborated. "He has indicated that he would like for me to go to Épernon and put his library there in order. After the war, that is. If I am unwilling to discuss it, he might grow angry—and curious."

Caroline held her breath, wondering if her

story would convince the viscount. She half wished he would rail at her, dragging the truth from her. Deceiving the viscount was becoming more difficult each time she was in his disturbing company. But, Caroline reminded herself for the hundredth time, her silence was buying protection for the people she cared about. She dared not forget Épernon's threats.

But the viscount appeared more interested in Épernon than in herself.

"Hmm. I wonder how your friend can be so sure his library, much less his *château*, is still standing. Or that he will possess it."

"I've no idea, my lord."

"Interesting. Nevertheless, if you'd rather not be pestered by the man, I can—"

"No!" she fairly gasped. "Please, my lord, you are very kind, but I need no help."

"Very well, as you wish. Only remember, my dear, I stand ready to be your ally should you need one." Changing the subject, the viscount asked, "Do you think your aunt would care to go to the theater this evening?"

"I'm sure I wouldn't know, my lord."

"I'll stop by and ask her, then. And what about Miss Pennington? Would she care to go? Lady Hensley and Augusta are to go as well."

His warm gaze made Caroline long to say yes. Silently, she cursed the comte.

"Thank you, my lord, but I don't wish to appear in society too often."

Rosemeade's brow arched, but he forbore to

point out that she had only gone out once. And had been dressed in costume then. He wondered again how she would appear in proper dress. But his face showed none of this.

"Another time, perhaps. One other thing: I am planning a small house party at Rosemeade for the month of July. I was hoping you and your aunt might be persuaded to join me."

With Lord Rosemeade's eyes on her, Caroline felt nearly powerless to refuse such a treat, but she knew she could not accept.

"You are very good, my lord, and I am tempted, but I cannot leave now."

"Why not? Why not take the time off? Lady Hensley and Augusta will be there. And Ferdie. Mrs. Stanton and Lady Hensley seem to get on famously."

"But, my lord, my work is not finished. It's true that I have organized most of the books, but I must label everything and make up a list of sorts." Caroline babbled on, anything to make Rosemeade forget his invitation. "Oh, yes, and I also wanted to ask you about ordering some engraved brass plates to label the shelves. It would be most helpful to members who are trying to locate a specific work. May I order them, my lord?"

"That goes without saying, Pennington. But I still wish for you to bring your aunt to Rosemeade. You once expressed the desire to see it."

"But truly, my lord, I cannot be gone so long."

"Then stay only a week or ten days. I can understand some reluctance, but surely a week cannot be too great a delay. At any rate, think on it. I will be back tomorrow." With this, the viscount rose from his chair and proceeded out the door.

"Why such haste, Caroline? The comte will understand if you are not ready. He can't eat you!"

"No, but I wouldn't wish to keep him waiting. It wouldn't be civil, Olivia," returned Caroline as she hastily donned her cloak, twitching the cuffs into place.

"Caroline, what is it? Is it that you are attracted to him?"

"Certainly not!"

"Then what does this comte hold over you that you scurry about at his beck and call?"

Caroline froze; she turned slowly, the very image of a disdainful young gentleman of fashion. But her supercilious manner did not intimidate her former governess in the least. Their eyes met. Livie never faltered.

Caroline sighed heavily, giving her friend a rueful grin.

"I am afraid if I repulse his friendship, he might try to retaliate and could discover my secret. I can't like him, but it is worth my efforts to keep on his good side."

Livie looked thoughtful. Then, delivering her best schoolmistress's smile, she murmured, "You must do as you see fit, dear."

"Good night, dearest Aunt. Have a good evening at the play, and remember: Not a word to the viscount!"

* * *

Épernon's weasel-faced smile made Caroline shiver as she entered his carriage.

"*Bonsoir*, Monsieur Pennington," said the comte, taking her hand in his.

"Épernon," growled Caroline, snatching her hand away.

"*Mon Dieu*, but we are out of sorts this evening."

"Just let me give you the information and take me home, Épernon."

"*Ah, non!* The information, *certainement*. But I feel we need to foster everyone's belief in our friendship. I have a box at the theater for this evening."

"The theater! I'm not going—"

A viselike grip closed on her arm; Épernon brought his face close to Caroline's, peering menacingly into her eyes. The comte's black eyes glowed in the light from the lantern on the side of the carriage.

"You will accompany me, and you will appear, at least, to enjoy yourself."

The carriage rolled to a stop.

"Ah, we are here. We will continue our most stimulating conversation inside, Charles," said the comte, his voice silky and self-assured.

She looked out at the many people close by and resigned herself to following his orders as long as they were in public.

Once seated in Épernon's box, they could both see and be seen well.

"A smile, *mon ami*," said the comte, nodding to an acquaintance in the pit.

Caroline fixed a smile on her face, inwardly cursing him. Just before the curtain rose for the first act, a stir across the way heralded the entrance of Rosemeade and his party. Caroline slipped lower in her seat.

"Your lovely aunt is here," said the comte, bowing to this lady. Livie returned a cool nod. "You didn't tell me your viscount would be here tonight."

"You didn't allow me enough time. Let's go!" she hissed.

She made as if to rise, but his hand restrained her. Glaring at one another, Caroline and the comte didn't realize the interest this slight altercation was generating.

The viscount's fist clenched, and Olivia whispered, "My lord, I'm worried. Could we discuss this later?"

He nodded. "Tomorrow morning."

The atmosphere at the breakfast table the next morning was strained. Olivia refrained from voicing the many questions crowding her worried mind. Caroline was on tenterhooks trying to steer Livie away from the topic of the previous evening.

As the silence lengthened, Caroline gulped a bite of toast and said, "That's a new gown, isn't it, Aunt?"

"Yes, I discovered an excellent dressmaker. You should visit her, my dear."

"Perhaps later, before we go home. Anyway, it's very becoming. You always look lovely in rose."

"Thank you, Caroline," Olivia said automatically.

Next it was Livie's turn to break the silence, and the question surfaced. "Did you enjoy the play, Caroline?"

"It was quite well done, I thought," replied Caroline, dreading the next query. But she was in for a surprise.

"I must agree, though I'm no expert, by any means. Well, I've some letters to write, and no doubt you'll be wishing to get to the club."

Olivia rose and walked with outward calm to the door. "Will you be dining at home this evening, dear?"

"I, uh, I don't know. I believe so," said Caroline.

"Good. I'll tell Mrs. Bates. Good-bye."

"Good-bye, Olivia," said Caroline, wrapped in confusion at her unexpected escape.

Promptly at ten o'clock, Bates admitted the viscount. Olivia sat by the window, the morning sun streaming onto the intricate pattern of her tatting. After bowing over her hand, Lord Rosemeade picked up one end of the fine cotton lace.

"You do exquisite work, Mrs. Stanton."

"Thank you, my lord. It is soothing, I think. I must pay close attention or I make a mistake. It keeps my mind occupied as well as my hands."

She motioned to the chair facing her own and the viscount seated himself.

"May I offer you some refreshment, my lord?"

"No, nothing, thank you. I just finished my breakfast. I would not attempt such an early call on very many ladies of my acquaintance, but you don't seem the lazy sort."

"I've been up for hours!" She laughed, adding, "Well, an hour or so. Thank you for inviting me last night. I enjoyed myself so. If only . . ."

"Yes, ma'am, if only. What are we going to do with your niece? I have warned her. I take it you have also had words with her on the subject."

"I thought if you would remonstrate . . ."

The viscount shook his head. "It would do no good," he replied.

Both parties sat silently, brows furrowed, staring into space, for several moments.

"Of course! How stupid of me!"

"What is it, my lord?" asked Olivia, leaning forward.

"You must persuade her that you wish—no, not wish to—that you are desperate to go to Rosemeade in July."

"Go to Rosemeade?" asked Olivia.

"So she didn't even tell you of my invitation," said the viscount quietly.

Olivia waited.

"I have invited some friends to my estate near Brighton for the month of July. Lady Lietchfield and Lady Hensley will be going, and I thought you and Caroline would enjoy it. London is so hot then, and I know Caroline would like to see my library at Rosemeade."

"It sounds delightful!"

"So I thought, but I'm afraid your niece was less than enthralled with the invitation when I extended it yesterday."

"Oh, dear. I wonder why," said Olivia, twisting her tatting between her finger and thumb distractedly.

"She said it was the work," explained the viscount doubtfully.

"I must apologize, my lord, if she was rude in any way. I . . ."

"No, ma'am, not rude. Unflattering, perhaps, but it never hurts to be reminded that one is not the center of the universe."

The twinkle in the viscount's eyes was pronounced, and Livie smiled at his nonsense despite her low spirits.

"Now, then, I extend the invitation to you. Do you suppose you might prevail upon that young chit to leave London—and the comte—and come to Rosemeade? I say," he added as an unwelcome suspicion assailed him, "you don't suppose she has formed a *tendre* for the man?"

"I wondered, too, but she says not. She seems almost frightened of him."

"Then it is even more imperative that we get her away from London. I feel responsible for her. If I hadn't allowed her to continue with this mad masquerade . . ."

"You mustn't blame yourself, my lord." Livie

squared her shoulders. "Very well, I shall try, but I can't feel sanguine about my chances for success. Caroline has always been very . . ."

"Obstinate," supplied the viscount. Livie smiled and nodded.

"Suppose Caroline thought you wanted to go, Mrs. Stanton."

"But I do," she insisted.

"I mean, that you are desperate to go. I don't wish to pry, Mrs. Stanton, but after Augusta's ball . . . That is, Mr. Farningham will also be at Rosemeade. Perhaps . . ."

He left the sentence hanging, and an unaccustomed blush spread across Olivia's cheeks.

"Yes, yes, I see. That might work. Not that it is true, but I think a small falsehood would be permissible in this case," said Olivia slowly.

"Excellent!" said the viscount as he rose to take his leave. "I shall expect to hear from you tomorrow, confirming our little plan."

"Thank you, my lord. You are too good."

"Rubbish!" he protested.

"It is not," said Olivia. "There are not many gentlemen who would concern themselves in the affairs of an employee, or of her aunt, for that matter. If Caroline is too wrapped up in herself that she does not recognize the honor you do us, you must know that I do, and I thank you."

"My pleasure, Mrs. Stanton. I like Caroline. I don't know yet what Épernon's game is—perhaps it is innocent enough—but I don't intend to stand by and let Caroline fall into his clutches.

You may set your mind at rest on that score, ma'am. Word of a Wyndridge."

He took her tiny hand, gave it a gentle, reassuring squeeze, then left her.

"Caroline, you are not trying, my dear. You must circulate more, listen more intently," said the comte softly.

"And what do I say when the viscount questions my lack of progress?" Caroline asked, waving a negligent hand about the library.

"If he should become suspicious, *mon ami,* Gustave might be induced to have a talk with his lordship."

Caroline seated herself, all bravado vanishing at this threat.

"Now, tomorrow I shall expect better, *n'est-ce pas?*" said the comte, moving toward the door.

"Yes," came the flat reply. Then, "One thing, Épernon."

"Oui?"

"I . . . I have an invitation."

"So?"

"It will take me away from London for a week or two," said Caroline.

"Where?"

"To Rosemeade, the viscount's estate near Brighton."

"Brighton, eh?"

Caroline nodded, but the comte appeared lost in thought. When he spoke again, Caroline's surprise was evident on her face.

"Accept your invitation, my dear. Stay as long

as you wish. Brighton will be filled with the fashionable and the military. What could be more ideal? I will be in touch."

With this, the comte slipped through the door, leaving Caroline to ponder his remarks.

After a splendid dinner of veal chops and raspberry trifle, Olivia mentioned the viscount's invitation. She didn't refer to his visit that morning but led Caroline to believe the invitation had been issued at the theater.

"Yes, he told me of it yesterday, too," said Caroline. "It slipped my mind." How easily the lies were rolling off her tongue these days, she thought.

"What do you think, Caroline? I must admit it is flattering, but our position being what it is . . ."

"Do you really wish to go, Livie?"

"Yes, Caroline. I . . . Did the viscount tell you who else would make up the house party?" asked Livie evasively.

"He said it would include Lady Lietchfield and Lady Hensley and ourselves."

"Also Ferdie Farningham," said Olivia, giving great care to her trifle.

"Ferdie Farningham? Oh, yes, I forgot." Caroline watched Olivia. Her friend was behaving strangely. Could it be? Farningham? She had known him years ago; perhaps they had been sweethearts. And, just perhaps, Olivia wanted to renew their relationship. She had never considered her companion a romantic, yet . . .

"And you wish to go, Olivia?"

"Why, yes, Caroline, I believe it would be amusing. Something to look back on when we are pounding sums into young ladies' heads. And I'd be getting you back into a dress rather than in breeches."

Caroline laughed, at ease knowing that she could grant her friend's desire. But then she recoiled at the realization that only the comte's permission allowed her to say yes; she clenched her fist beneath the table in frustration.

"When do we leave?" she managed to ask.

"You mean you'll go?" asked Olivia, amazed at the ease of her victory.

"I don't see any harm in it. The library at White's will wait."

"I had no idea you'd made so much progress, but I'm glad we can go. Do you think we should go shopping before we leave?"

Caroline laughed, then struck a disdainful masculine pose, which looked odd in her gown.

"Just like a female!"

Chapter Seven

One week later, Caroline and Olivia were installed in the well-sprung landau that the viscount had set aside to convey them to Rosemeade.

Rosemeade had been in the guidebooks for many years because of its rose gardens and history. The father of the present viscount had added an impressive system of succession houses that produced hundreds of varieties of plants year-round.

Robert Wyndridge, the present Lord Rosemeade, had added five acres of fruit trees, but other than this, the gardeners' routines had remained unchanged.

When the carriage passed the gatehouse, Caroline and Olivia peered out eagerly, hoping for a glimpse of the house. They were disappointed. The drive was the width of three carriages, covered not with gravel but with crushed seashells, giving evidence to the fact that the sea was only eight miles away. On either side, the way was lined with great hedges fifteen feet high, obscuring the view of the estate grounds and the house. They continued up this road for one mile.

"I see the end of the shrubs finally, Aunt," Caroline said petulantly. "I was beginning to think it would be dark before we came out into the open again."

"Oh, look, Caroline." Olivia sighed as the house came into view.

The scene before them was breathtaking, but

not awesome. It appeared intimate and inviting. The house was set on a perfectly manicured lawn. To the left, among several huge oak trees, was a charming gazebo. To the right, winding past the house, the drive was lined with more oak trees.

But it was the house itself that made the scene entrancing. It was constructed of rose-colored quartz, or so it appeared to Caroline. The setting sun filtered through the trees, striking the stone and mortar with a startling effect: the stones appeared translucent, soaking up the pink of the sunset.

Caroline mentioned this to Olivia, who smiled. "If you had read the guidebook, my dear Caroline, you would know that the Wyndridge who built the house selected the stones for that quality. It says the effect is also astounding at sunrise, for the stones appear a pale yellow."

"Really? I shall rise early one morning just to see that!"

The carriage pulled up under the covered entranceway on the right side of the house. The coach door was opened, and Caroline took the footman's hand, then turned to assist Olivia. Stretching in an unladylike fashion, Caroline noticed that only a stone footpath led from the drive to the front of the house. It was this that gave the impression of an unrelieved sea of green surrounding the house.

A formidable-looking butler appeared at the door. Caroline swallowed hard; this individual looked to be much higher in the instep than his master. But upon hearing his kindly tones, Caroline relaxed.

"Mrs. Stanton, Miss Pennington. His lordship is out hunting. I am Sanders, his lordship's butler. Welcome to Rosemeade."

"Thank you, Sanders," said Caroline.

"Your rooms are ready, ladies. I'm certain you wish to rest before dinner. His lordship said to tell you we keep country hours here. Dinner is at seven."

With this, the butler turned and led them down a long, wide corridor lined with armored breastplates, crossbows, longbows, rapiers, and heavy swords and shields. The hall opened into a large, well-lighted foyer. To the left stood huge double doors; this was the front of the house. To the right rose a staircase wide enough for two mail coaches to pass easily; it split at the first landing, curving majestically upward in opposite directions.

Passing down one corridor into another, Sanders at last paused at one door.

"Mrs. Stanton, your room. Miss Pennington will be in the next room. The bellpull is by the door. Please ring if you require anything. I shall send a maid up to fetch you both twenty minutes before dinner, if that will be convenient."

"Fine, Sanders. Thank you."

"How elegant you look, Mrs. Stanton," said the viscount as his two guests entered the salon.

And how handsome you are, my lord, thought Caroline. The viscount wore a very proper gray coat, but in place of his starched cravat he sported a yellow silk neckerchief.

"Thank you, my lord."

"I hope Sanders has made you comfortable."

"Yes, my room is delightful, and the view is breathtaking."

The viscount smiled broadly. "My father would have loved to receive that compliment, Mrs. Stanton. He always took a special interest in the gardens, whereas I merely allow Reynolds, our head gardener, to continue in his usual vein. He is quite talented and would not welcome interference from an amateur such as myself."

"I'm sure you underestimate yourself, my lord."

"No, Mrs. Stanton, not a bit of it," he replied.

All this time Caroline had been standing like a statue, unable to participate in this exchange, for she was so astounded by the change in their host's appearance.

Or was it a change in the viscount, wondered Caroline, that made her long to lay her hand on his sleeve? If only her circumstances were different, if Épernon weren't blackmailing her, perhaps she could explore the reasons behind her quickened pulse.

Rosemeade noticed his other guest's bemused state and said, "I trust I haven't offended either of you by my casual attire. Since the others will not arrive until tomorrow, I thought you would forgive my informal dress, since we are dining almost *en famille.*"

"We are not offended in the least, my lord. Are we, Caroline, dear?" prodded Olivia.

"Uh, no, not at all. You must forgive my staring, my lord, but I have never seen you wear a Belcher necktie," commented Caroline, trying to explain away her silence. What was the matter with her? she thought.

"Caroline!" exclaimed Olivia.

The viscount's laugh rang out clearly. "It is sheer laziness that's made me wear it tonight."

Caroline turned beet-red, feeling the joke was on her somehow. Rosemeade sensed her chagrin and set out to make her feel comfortable once again. But though she could lose herself in conversation for a moment, her eyes kept wandering back to the viscount.

"I hope you enjoy the pheasant in sour cream. Our cook knows it to be one of my favorites," the viscount said as the footmen presented the first course.

"It is very good, my lord. Your cook's secret recipe, perhaps?" said Miss Stanton.

"I don't know if she considers it secret. Would you like to have it?"

"Very much, thank you."

"But I doubt Miss Pennington would approve," teased the viscount.

Caroline's eyes dropped to her plate, and she began eating the pheasant, commenting on its excellence.

Caroline struggled to keep her mind on the topics at hand, determined to mask her distraction as mouth-watering lamb, ham with raisin sauce, pâté, Brussels sprouts with green grapes, Rhenish creams, and sherried baked bananas paraded across her plate.

As for the viscount, he studied his young guest also, but less obtrusively. He had seen her dressed in a proper gown before, but this time the effect was unsettling. She had appeared dull and studious in her men's garments with her hair scraped back. But in her jonquil gown, her willowy figure was alluring, and the dark curls framing her face were seductive. Were they as soft as they looked? he wondered.

He quickly excused himself after dinner, leaving the ladies at the door of the salon.

"What on earth is wrong with you, Caroline?" chided Olivia.

"Wrong? What should be wrong, Aunt?"

"I'm sure I don't know. I only hope you are not becoming ill. I know how you hate having to call in a doctor."

"I'm only tired, Olivia. Don't fret so."

The viscount entered, carrying a rather dusty bottle in one hand.

"I knew Sanders would find it! A bottle of my mother's favorite sherry, Mrs. Stanton. I'm hopeful it will meet with your approval," he explained, gingerly wiping off the dust before opening the bottle.

After presenting a full glass to Olivia, he splashed a bit of the amber liquid into another glass and offered it to Caroline. Filling a snifter with brandy for himself, he raised his glass to the ladies.

"To my delightful visitors. May you enjoy your stay at Rosemeade."

Next, Caroline raised her glass to the viscount, saying, "To our host, Lord Rosemeade."

Olivia tasted her sherry, nodding her approval.

"Tomorrow morning, Caroline, I shall take you into my library and let you loose. You'll no doubt revel in the freedom to explore instead of cataloguing."

"I look forward to it, my lord."

"Good. For tonight, perhaps you would play for us, Mrs. Stanton."

"Oh, no, my lord. Truly, you don't wish me to do so! My playing is hardly passable. Caroline, why don't you play for us? You are much better than I."

The viscount looked surprised. Somehow, skill at the pianoforte seemed too tame a talent for the daring Miss Pennington. Here again it appeared he would have to reassess his opinion of the girl.

Caroline took her place at the instrument, played a few tentative chords, and then launched into a sonata by Haydn. From that she glided into Beethoven's *Moonlight* Sonata.

"Bravo!" exclaimed the viscount, applauding. "I had no idea you were so talented."

"It isn't so much, my lord," she protested, seating herself beside Olivia on the settee. His praise pleased her, and Caroline found it difficult to refrain from grinning.

"You've not been constrained to listen to countless so-called talented young ladies at house parties or you wouldn't say that."

Caroline's smile faded as she contemplated how dissimilar her life had been from the viscount's. They came from different worlds.

"Mrs. Stanton, would you care to play a game? We could play three-handed—"

"No, my lord, you must hold me excused, but you two play," said Olivia earnestly. "I haven't the patience for cards this evening. Not when I am tired. I'll just work on my embroidery."

"If you are positive . . . ?" said the viscount, and Livie nodded. "How about it, Caroline? A rematch at backgammon?"

"Excellent, my lord."

They were both thoughtful players, taking the time to work out the best possible move with each throw of the die. While the viscount studied the board, Caroline continued to study the viscount.

She still could not identify the change in his appearance. Perhaps, she reasoned with herself, it is only that he is more at ease here than in London. But that seemed irrational. He was always self-assured. And she had seen him in doeskin breeches before, so that was not new. The gray coat, however, was new to her.

"Your turn, Caroline," said the viscount. She jumped.

"Sorry, my lord. I must be more tired than I thought."

He gave her his crooked grin. "I thought I was winning too easily. You're not up to your usual game!"

Caroline redoubled her efforts to concentrate. But her mind persisted in its wanderings. She looked up again to find the viscount's steel-gray eyes, now questioning, on her. His eyes! she thought. His jacket is just the color of his eyes. And so was the salon, she realized with a start.

It was the perfect setting. Had the viscount selected the gray wallpaper with the tiny maroon and white flowers just to match his eyes? How vain!

"I believe we'd best call it quits," said the viscount.

"Have you won already?" asked Livie, looking up from her needlework.

"No, but it's of no use to continue. I may as well be playing by myself," said Rosemeade, an amused gleam turning his eyes to blue-gray.

The words sunk into Caroline's drifting thoughts, and she apologized. "I'm sorry, my lord. When I'm sleepy, I just can't concentrate."

"I noticed, my dear. However, we will have time for another game tomorrow," said the viscount, rising from his chair.

"My lord, I've no wish to pry, but who decorated this room? It is quite handsome."

"Do you like it, Caroline? It has always been a favorite of mine. My mother selected everything, and I can't bring myself to change it, though the draperies and carpet are becoming worn. It is the exact color of her eyes," he concluded.

"And of yours," murmured Caroline.

Rosemeade smiled. "Yes, that's true. Now, off

to bed with you. A good night's sleep and you'll be your old self again, child."

Curled up in the cozy, four-poster bed, Caroline fell asleep at once, dreaming of a tall gentleman with chestnut hair and gray eyes that melted to blue as he watched her enter his room.

A timid knock heralded the entrance of Olivia the next morning.

"Aunt, no one would ever guess you are not a debutante once again," said Caroline gallantly. "Has Mr. Farningham arrived yet?"

Livie's complexion turned a becoming shade of pink that matched her morning gown.

"What nonsense, Caroline! I am thirty-six years old and a confirmed spinster."

Caroline chuckled. "By my count, you will not be thirty-six until August."

"That's as it may be, young lady," said Olivia. "Now, let me have a look at you."

Caroline turned around, looking over her shoulder to gauge her friend's reaction. Livie smiled, well satisfied with her charge's appearance.

"It is so pleasant to have you always dressed as befits your sex." She gave a delicate shudder as she recalled Caroline in breeches.

"It is reassuring to me," said Caroline as she regarded her image in the mirror, "to know I can still look feminine, even without my hair."

Livie came to stand behind her. "I believe I prefer your hair in short ringlets, my dear. It is certainly more fashionable."

"Nevertheless, I plan to let it grow out as soon as we get home."

"We're not home yet," said Livie. "I've been meaning to speak to you about something that's troubling me."

"I'm listening," said Caroline.

"You mustn't let the viscount's offer of hospitality and friendship lead you to believe there's anything more there."

"What ever can you mean?" Caroline picked up a comb and began to drag it ruthlessly through her curls.

"I saw the way you looked at his lordship last night."

Caroline gave an unconvincing laugh. "Really, Livie, you could not be more mistaken! I was merely tired."

"Perhaps, but I hope you won't be angry with me for being frank. It is just that our situation here is so unorthodox. Lord Rosemeade treats you with a familiarity at times that would be considered impertinent. I fear he may forget himself. It would never do."

Caroline moved to the edge of the bed and stared out the window. Tears filled her eyes, but her voice was steady.

"Never fear, Livie. His lordship seems to regard me as a younger sibling—brother or sister, it doesn't matter which. Of course, it makes for interesting conversations; no topic is prohibited since I'm just a child in his eyes."

Caroline took a deep breath and added, "You go on down to breakfast. I shall follow shortly."

* * *

"This is the animal I was telling you about, Caroline," said the viscount, pointing out a rather ugly roan trotting along the fence.

"Holier Than Thou?"

"That's he. But my favorite is Dover—I raised him from a colt."

"Which is he?" asked Caroline naïvely.

The viscount shook his head. "You've a lot to learn about horses, Caroline. Dover is in the south pasture. He's a real beauty, though Ferdie holds that he's all show and no bottom."

"Truer word was never spoken, Robert!" exclaimed Mr. Farningham, appearing behind them. He extended his hand to Caroline. "Servant, Miss Pennington."

"I'm very glad to see you again, Mr. Farningham."

"Here, now, no need for the 'Mr.' Call me Ferdie."

And to the viscount's surprise, Caroline laughed, saying, "Very well, Ferdie."

"Where's that beast Dover?" asked Ferdie of the viscount.

"Always so subtle, that's Ferdie!" observed Rosemeade, smiling down at his stocky friend. "South pasture with my new mare, Greydawn."

"A shame to waste her on that overgrown mongrel, Robert!"

"Now see here, Ferdie, may I remind you I bred that 'overgrown mongrel.' "

"Harumph! No need to get on your high ropes,

Robert!" said Ferdie, winking at Caroline. "Time will tell. Time will tell."

With this ominous warning, Ferdie strolled past the duo at the fence to confer with his man about caring for his matched bays.

"I wonder at times why I put up with Ferdie," muttered the viscount.

"Because he's a friend," offered Caroline.

Rosemeade smiled. "Would you care to see the library now? I've some work to do, so you may have the run of it until luncheon. I realize I may need a crowbar to pry you out, but that can't be helped."

"I believe you two are acquainted?" asked the viscount innocently as he and Ferdie strolled into the small dining room for the noon meal.

"Yes, my lord, Mr. Farningham and I are old friends," responded Livie.

"Excellent! Now, Ferdie, you sit over there by Mrs. Stanton. Caroline, you sit by me; I want your opinion of my library."

"Of course, my lord," said Caroline, slipping into the chair indicated and trying to suppress a grin as Ferdie sat down and immediately claimed Olivia's attention.

Half an hour passed in this manner with Caroline and Rosemeade speaking to the engrossed couple on occasion but receiving only monosyllables in reply.

Finally, the viscount rose and announced his intention to drive down by the south pasture with Caroline to see his stallion.

"You do that, Robert," said Ferdie, turning back to Olivia.

"Ferdie, why don't you take Mrs. Stanton for a stroll in the rose garden?"

"Would you like that, Livie?" asked Mr. Farningham eagerly.

"That would be lovely, Ferdie," came the reply, and they both rose and left the room.

Rosemeade rolled his eyes heavenward, and Caroline broke into uncontrollable giggles. The viscount's booming laugh mingled with hers.

When he had recovered, the viscount said, "I don't know if I can stomach playing Cupid. I'm certain it's bad for the digestion!"

Early in the afternoon Lady Hensley and Lady Lietchfield arrived. Their abigails and trunks appeared first, so all was in readiness when mother and daughter bustled into Rosemeade. They were ushered to their rooms at once and left to recuperate from their arduous journey until dinner.

As Augusta entered the drawing room, the viscount greeted her warmly.

Looking into her eyes, he said, "The wait was well worth it, my dear. You're ravishing."

"Thank you, Robert. I wonder what outrageous compliment you shall offer me by morning?" She laughed, freeing her hands and joining Miss Stanton on the sofa. She greeted Caroline and gave Ferdie a tolerant "How d'you do."

"Mother will be down shortly. Her abigail has mislaid a glove, and when I left, a frantic search was underway," Augusta informed them, her blue eyes twinkling.

Everyone laughed, even Caroline, though she felt a slight pang of jealousy whenever she looked at Lady Lietchfield. No one, she thought, should be that lovely! The bright blue eyes, golden curls, and exquisite figure were hard enough. But Caroline could not help liking her. She was open and friendly, unlike so many ladies of the ton.

"Lady Hensley, welcome. I trust you found your glove," said the viscount as Augusta's mother appeared in the doorway.

"Yes, dear boy, thank you. It was not even the girl who lost it; I had stuffed it into a reticule and forgotten about it."

She glided over to Miss Stanton, and her daughter vacated her seat, allowing her mother to sit down.

"Was your journey comfortable, ma'am?" asked Miss Stanton.

Lady Hensley made a moue. "Tolerable, but hardly comfortable. Don't you find that as one grows older and has made the same journey many times before that it is the boredom that wears one down?"

Olivia looked surprised but agreed politely. Only a week earlier, she had placed herself in the same category as Lady Hensley. Now, for some inexplicable reason, Olivia was shocked to think the elderly widow (who was at least fifteen years her senior) considered herself a contemporary. Involuntarily, Olivia's gaze drifted to the hearth where Ferdie lounged. Until a few days ago, she had accepted her place on the shelf. Now . . .

"Mrs. Stanton?" repeated Lady Hensley.

"What? Oh, I'm sorry. What did you ask?"

Lady Hensley smiled, for she had noticed where Olivia's attention had wandered. She recalled the dance Olivia Stanton and Farningham had shared at her ball.

"I asked if you arrived yesterday."

"Yes, yes, we did."

"My lord, dinner is served."

"Very good, Sanders." The viscount offered his arm to Lady Hensley. Augusta took his other arm, leaning against him. Ferdie appeared at Olivia's side. Caroline would have been forgotten if the viscount had not turned and prompted Ferdie.

Rosemeade sat at the head of the table, while Lady Hensley played hostess at the other end. Augusta sat on the viscount's right, Caroline on his left. Ferdie and Olivia had to content themselves with sitting across from each other. Conversation became general.

Leaning toward Caroline, the petite Augusta whispered, "Your aunt and Mr. Farningham appear very taken with each other."

"They're old friends," explained Caroline.

"Friends? No, Miss Pennington, you mark me: it is much more serious than that!"

Caroline, glancing down at Lady Hensley, realized the older lady had taken over the role of Cupid and was enjoying herself immensely.

"Robert, how is your brother? You haven't

mentioned him," Augusta asked next, resting her hand lightly on his forearm.

A cloud passed over the viscount's features.

"I've no idea how he is, Augusta. It's been months since I've had word of him. His friends say he received orders and left. But that was over three months ago."

"I'm so sorry, Robert."

"How long has he been in the army, my lord?" asked Caroline.

The viscount managed a smile for his young guest. "Garrett's been in for the past three years. My old regiment."

That was a surprise. Caroline hadn't realized the viscount had served in the army. She couldn't imagine him taking orders from anyone.

"What regiment is that, my lord?"

"Second Division. I was in the earliest Peninsula campaigns. Then my father died, and I felt I had to resign. But Garrett, who was twenty-two at the time, soon talked me into allowing him to join. He's a captain now."

"I didn't know he'd advanced so," said Augusta.

"Yes. You know, I wanted him to go into the Foreign Office. He speaks Prussian, Spanish, and French fluently, as well as a smattering of Russian. But he wanted the army."

"Like his big brother, no doubt," commented Augusta.

The viscount smiled at her. "I suppose. Even so, with his talents, he has often been sent on missions to our allies, acting as courier and liaison. A very dangerous assignment." Caroline recalled the viscount's comments about spies around London. Garrett's mission must have been a matter of espionage.

"You must be very proud of him, my lord," said Caroline.

"I am," said Rosemeade, adding, "I only wish I knew where he was."

This forlorn comment caused Caroline to reflect on her own efforts at spying. What if the insignificant information she had passed on had harmed Garrett Wyndridge in some way? The viscount would never forgive her.

The gentlemen remained only a brief time over their port and soon rejoined the ladies. Augusta was playing the pianoforte as they entered. Lady Hensley, upon spying Ferdie Farningham, patted the seat beside her on the settee. Since Olivia was on the other end of this, Ferdie obliged willingly.

The viscount stood back, surveying his drawing room. A small but congenial group, he concluded. It was too bad his friends Julian and Abby had already taken a house in Brighton, but they would be available for outings. It promised to be a pleasant visit.

Polite applause greeted Augusta as she completed the melody she was playing.

"Miss Pennington, why don't you play and let Lady Lietchfield sing. She has a lovely voice," suggested the viscount.

"Of course, my lord," said Caroline.

"Now, Robert," protested Augusta, "I shan't sing unless I can persuade you to join me."

"Very well."

Thus, Caroline endured a very miserable evening seated at the pianoforte, Lord Rosemeade standing on one side and Lady Lietchfield on the other. The trio executed two romantic ballads flawlessly while Caroline's spirits sank.

They made an early night of it, for the travelers were weary. Caroline retired, thankful for the time alone to try to forget the way Lady Lietchfield had gazed so at the viscount all evening.

But sleep was impossible. Thinking she would benefit from an hour or so in the viscount's extensive library, Caroline threw on a dressing gown, picked up her candle, and let herself out.

She soon found an early version of Pope's *The Rape of the Lock* in a copy of Lintot's *Miscellaneous Poems and Translations by several hands* and settled onto the leather couch.

The clock was chiming six when she woke with a start. Gray light was filtering through the curtains. She retrieved the gutted candle and, taking up the forgotten volume, made her way back upstairs.

Rounding the corner of the hall, she thought she saw the viscount. She ducked into a doorway until the form passed, seeming to end at a door across from hers.

Caroline slipped into her chamber in a trance. Even if she hadn't known who occupied the chamber opposite her own, she could guess now:

Augusta, Lady Lietchfield. So this had been the entire purpose of the house party; it had nothing to do with her.

Out loud, she whispered, "He's in love with her."

Then she burst into tears.

Rosemeade's guests enjoyed a late breakfast the next morning. The viscount and Ferdie, who had eaten earlier, entertained the ladies. But Caroline slept on.

"What shall we do this afternoon, Robert?" asked Lady Hensley.

"There is some fine scenery if you wish to take a carriage ride."

"No, a long carriage ride for me today is out of the question," declared Lady Hensley.

"Would you like to go to Brighton, Mama?"

"Hmm. What do you think, Mrs. Stanton? Shall we go to Brighton?"

"I'd like that," said Olivia.

"To go shopping, no doubt," grumbled Ferdie.

"How else can we ladies contrive to dazzle you with our beauty?" asked Augusta.

Ferdie's reply was cut short by the viscount, who signaled to a footman.

"Have an abigail go and wake Miss Pennington."

The ladies repaired to their rooms to change for the outing. The viscount opened the door to his own chamber. A maid appeared and bobbed a curtsy.

"Yes?"

"Please, my lord, I went to wake Miss Pennington, but she wasn't in her room."

"Very well." He thought for a moment, then hurried down the corridor.

The viscount paused as he entered the library, his eyes taking a moment to adjust to the gloomy room. Thinking the chamber empty, he turned to go when his eye caught a slight movement.

There she is, thought Rosemeade, just as I suspected. He crossed the floor and stood looking down at the sleeping figure on the sofa.

Caroline was curled into a tight ball, her wool wrapper tucked around her feet, her cheek resting on her hand. Her brow was furrowed as though concentrating on some sticky problem.

Rosemeade smiled and stretched out his hand, his fingers touching her soft cheek. She sighed.

"Caroline, are you awake?" he whispered as he kneeled by her side.

The viscount's voice intruded into her dreams. Caroline's brow cleared as she smiled and stretched her legs.

"Wake up, my dear," said Rosemeade, wondering at the rush of tenderness he felt. He dismissed it; she was only a child.

Bleary-eyed, Caroline looked up to see him peering at her.

"Robert!" she yelped, her voice deep and gravelly. She sat up at once and tucked her slippered feet beneath the wrapper.

Rosemeade cleared his throat, impatient with himself and his guest. She had no right to disturb him by looking so vulnerable.

"Easy, Miss Pennington. We were worried about you. It's almost noon," continued the viscount, striding to the windows and opening the curtains without so much as another glance at the sofa. Caroline ran a hand through her curls and swung her feet to the floor.

Glaring at his lordship, she snapped, "I do apologize, my lord. I was up late reading and fell asleep. I'm surprised to see you awake so early."

Without realizing it, he irritated her even further by saying cheerfully, "I never sleep late. I wondered if you wished to accompany us into Brighton. The ladies have expressed their desire to visit the shops. When do ladies not want to shop?" he added. "I wondered if you'd enjoy touring the town."

Hiding her annoyance, Caroline said, "Very good, my lord. Give me twenty minutes, and I'll be dressed."

"Do you need any help?" he asked without thinking.

As she flashed him a look of disdain, he added, "That is, I could send a maid up to you."

"No, thank you, my lord. I can manage," Caroline said with a great deal more calm than she felt.

"As you wish. No need to hurry a great deal; everyone else is changing," said Rosemeade as he retreated to the door. He walked slowly down the corridor, grappling with a peculiar puzzle.

"My lord this, my lord that," he mimicked to himself. "But it's Robert when she's asleep." And why is she so snappish? Half the time she's so damn meek and subservient; the other half, as sharp-tongued as a shrew.

No solution presented itself, for the viscount, despite his experience with women, never looked inward to explain his guest's mood swings.

So, even as he rejoined the others, the viscount had no answer to his questions. Putting the matter aside, he presented a smiling visage to the group in the salon.

"Ferdie, I'm afraid Miss Pennington will take too long getting ready, and I see the ladies have been unusually prompt in presenting themselves. Why don't you escort our lovely companions on their shopping expedition and meet us at, say, three o'clock at the Strand. There is a new shop there that sells ices. Miss Pennington wants to see a bit of the countryside, anyway. We'll follow as soon as she's ready."

Ferdie looked mildly disgruntled, but as he turned back and saw Olivia, he agreed to the plan.

"I'd be honored," he replied, causing Rosemeade to grin.

On Augusta's lovely brow the viscount discovered a frown. She was unhappy with him, and with just cause, perhaps. He had invited her to Rosemeade, and Augusta was no doubt angry at being foisted off on Ferdie, whom she barely tolerated.

However, Caroline was also his guest, and as host, he couldn't very well leave the child behind. Augusta would get over it.

But the viscount was faulty in his judgment. Augusta's frown was the outward sign of a very different emotion. Jealousy, like a fast-growing vine, was entwining itself around her heart.

"Mount up, Miss Pennington! I promise you, Morgan will be as gentle as a mother with a newborn colt. She wouldn't dream of dumping you on the ground," said the viscount.

"Dream or not, you and I know that my skills as a rider are lacking," grumbled Caroline as she stared at the unfamiliar sidesaddle. She gathered the skirt of her new riding habit and wondered how things could get any worse. With her host's help, she mounted the neat gray mare.

"I thought you meant to drive to Brighton, Lord Rosemeade. Just how long does it take to get there on horseback, my lord?"

"Here now, Miss Pennington. When you were half asleep, you called me Robert. Surely you can do so now. After all, you call Ferdie by his given name."

"I suppose so, my . . . Robert." She repressed the desire to tell him he had long been Robert in her thoughts.

"Not so difficult, was it? Now, to answer your question. By direct route, about an hour. But I thought we'd take the scenic route, across Rosemeade, if that's to your liking."

"Certainly, my lord. I only hope this horse is agreeable," said Caroline.

The viscount's hoot of laughter startled Caroline's mare, causing her to sidestep. Caroline grabbed the pommel and managed to stay mounted.

"Gentle as a mother with a newborn colt, eh?" she mumbled.

The viscount, unable to hide his mirth, kicked his horse and cantered away. Caroline took a deep breath and followed. Even mounted sidesaddle, she found, to her surprise, that the mare was much easier to handle than the gelding, Skipper. Also, she reasoned, the mare was much smaller, so she wouldn't have as far to fall. Little by little, she began to relax.

Before she realized what was happening, the viscount's horse was sailing over a three-foot fence just ahead of her. Unable to pull up, Caroline leaned forward as the mare gathered herself and left the ground, taking the fence easily and landing gently on the other side. Caroline opened her eyes wide in wonder. Even in the sidesaddle, she'd managed to keep her seat.

"Did you see that, Robert? Did you see that?" Caroline exclaimed as she pulled the mare to a halt, patting the glossy neck furiously.

"First-rate, my dear. Your form needs work, of course, but we can manage that," he replied. His mild praise caused Caroline to blush with pleasure.

"You know, this riding business isn't so bad after all, Robert. As long as there's a jump here or there. Can you teach me to jump something higher?" she demanded.

"Not so fast! Is this the same Caroline Pennington who had to be forced to learn to ride?"

"Don't be facetious, my lord," she said haughtily. "I still don't trust horses, but that jump was exhilarating. I should like to learn how to jump better."

On impulse, Caroline kicked the mare's side and sent her away again. Shaking his head, the viscount followed.

"And did you ladies leave anything in the shops?" Rosemeade asked as he seated Augusta in the pastry shop.

"Not much!" said Ferdie, who had had enough feminine company for one afternoon.

"Don't listen to him, Robert. We were very good, absolutely frugal!" said Lady Hensley.

"Yes, indeed! That is why I shall have to sit with packages on my knees all the way home," continued Ferdie. "Robert, old boy, I don't suppose you'd—"

"Ferdie," said Olivia.

"Oh, never mind, it was just a thought."

"Robert, we are going to the assembly tomorrow night, aren't we?"

"If you wish, Augusta. I find them rather dull, but if everyone wants to go, so be it," said the viscount.

"Of course we'll attend the assembly. Why else come to Brighton at this time of the year!" said Lady Hensley, forestalling any further discussion.

After sampling the ices, Lady Hensley said, "I propose we leave now, Robert. You young people are such gadabouts, but I must rest if we are entertaining tonight."

"Certainly, my lady, though adding one couple to our dinner table is hardly entertaining, especially when they are old friends like Julian and Abby," said Rosemeade.

"Mama, you know you've twice the stamina of any of us," declared the lady's daughter with a laugh.

"Nevertheless, we have been gone all day. It's time we were returning."

All this was spoken as the group moved out of the ice parlor. Caroline was smiling at this typical mother-daughter exchange when a rough-looking man in homespun crossed the road just in front of them. He stopped to let them pass, tipping his hat to the ladies.

Caroline would not even have glanced his way if he hadn't cleared his throat loudly. She found herself staring into the menacing eyes of Gustave Thibault. She stumbled, and he reached out and grabbed her arm to steady her. As he did so, he slipped a folded piece of paper into her palm and closed her fingers around it.

"Careful, young lady. You would not wish to fall and hurt yourself, eh?"

Terror-stricken, her first instinct was to run, but Caroline caught the viscount's curious gaze on her.

"Thank you, sir," she said, and hurried to catch up with Olivia.

The Scandalous Miss

* * *

"Caroline," said the viscount as they rode side by side in front of the carriage. "Are you in any kind of trouble? If you are, I—"

"Trouble, my lord? What trouble could I possibly have?"

"I'm sure I don't know, but something frightened you."

He's hitting too close to the truth, thought Caroline.

"You mean when I started to fall. Yes, that rather shook me up. By the way, who are your other guests this evening, my lord?"

The viscount grimaced at the "my lord." Really, any time Miss Pennington wanted to put him off, she just threw in a few "my lords." But the viscount took his cue.

"They are two old friends, the Earl of Aberley and his wife Abby, an American. I was at Eton with the earl, and later Cambridge, so he is hardly your contemporary, but I believe you'll like them both. Almost everyone does, though Julian is a bit of a hothead."

"I'm surprised you and he survived your friendship, my lord," said Caroline with wide-eyed innocence.

Rosemeade smiled dangerously. "You're a quick-witted baggage! Let's see if you dare ride as quickly. I'll race you home!"

Saying this, he drove his heels into his horse's sides and was away like a shot. Caroline took off after him, bending low over Morgan's neck and speaking softly to her. The mare's ears flattened as she caught sight of the viscount's gelding and she gathered speed, slowly narrowing the gap.

Leaving the road behind, they crossed a green meadow, both horses slowing slightly to take the stone wall. The stableyard came into view and instinctively both horses lengthened their strides.

With the mare's nose almost touching the gelding's rump, Caroline eased back on the reins. The game little horse resisted at first but then began to slow her pace, entering the stableyard at a sedate trot.

Flushed with excitement, Caroline leaped to the ground, throwing her arms around the mare's foam-flecked neck and stroking her vigorously.

"I knew I'd make a horsewoman of you yet, Caroline!" said the viscount.

"She's a right one, isn't she!" answered Caroline, letting the groom lead the mare off to be cooled down.

"That she is. Do you have a place for her in Cambridge?" asked Rosemeade on impulse.

"A place?"

"Yes, I'd like to give you the mare, if you've a place to keep her."

"Oh, no, my lord. I couldn't accept such a gift."

"Why not? She's had two colts; the last one nearly killed her. She's of no use as a brood mare, but she is a good hack. I'd like for someone to have her who would enjoy her, use her."

Caroline hesitated, then reiterated, "No, my

lord. You are too generous. I couldn't accept such a gift." But even as she repeated her refusal, she looked after the mare. What a comfort Morgan would be once I go back home, she thought. Having her would help me to remember this afternoon.

The viscount didn't press her. He would bide his time.

Long after the dinner that evening, and after the congenial group had separated, Caroline, Ferdie, and the viscount sat in silence in the salon. Everyone else had retired, but Caroline had elected to stay up; she felt restless each time her fingers touched the note in the pocket of her gown.

The comte was in Brighton; she wasn't really surprised. He had ordered her to meet him in her guise as Charles Pennington at the assembly the next evening. Caroline took another sip of her sherry, wishing she could forget about the comte.

The thoughts whirled in her mind: the note, the comte, the deception, the viscount. It was at this point she became confused. She did hate to deceive him, but after all, she had been careful to render the information she gave Épernon useless by changing it slightly.

Her conscience would let her do no less. And if Épernon discovered this ruse? She shuddered.

"Are you cold, my dear?" asked Rosemeade.

"No, my lord," Caroline responded. The sound of his voice alone warmed her.

Ferdie expelled a loud sigh and proceeded to

snore gently. The viscount smiled lazily at his sleeping friend.

"What did you think of the earl and his bride?" he asked Caroline.

"His bride?" she queried. "With a child six years old?"

"It's rare, but sometimes when couples marry, the wife remains a bride. I always get that feeling with Julian and Abby. My parents were the same."

Caroline nodded. "I see what you mean. I intercepted one look between them . . ."

"Disconcerting, isn't it? As though you've intruded on a very intimate exchange."

"Hmm."

"I wonder what it would be like to care about someone that deeply," said Rosemeade.

This observation caused Caroline to glance at the viscount. What about Augusta? she wanted to ask.

Then she frowned, recalling the shadowy figure she had seen in the hall the night before.

Had he really been visiting Lady Lietchfield? She had been so certain, but their behavior at dinner had been friendly rather than intimate.

Yet if it hadn't been the viscount, then who else could have been stealing down the corridor so early?

Ferdie Farningham snorted, causing Caroline to eye him suspiciously.

Chapter Eight

The morning brought rain, and everyone chose his or her own means of escape. The viscount was closeted with his bailiff in his workroom. Lady Hensley and Lady Lietchfield discussed fashion over their needlework. Olivia held her tatting but made little progress. Ferdie had forgone the stables and sat by her side, conversing quietly.

"Where is Miss Pennington?" asked Lady Lietchfield as they converged around the dining table for luncheon.

"In the library, no doubt. I'll fetch her," said Olivia.

"No need, Mrs. Stanton. I'll get her," volunteered his lordship. "Go ahead and serve, Sanders."

The door opened and closed without a sound. Caroline didn't look up, so engrossed was she in the volume she held.

"Luncheon, Caroline," Rosemeade whispered. She jumped.

"Robert!"

"Sorry to startle you. What are you reading?"

"A neat little novel. Or perhaps, novella; it's so short," she answered, extending the book for his inspection.

"This was Garrett's, one of his favorites," said the viscount quietly, smoothing the pages.

"You mean 'is' one of Garrett's," Caroline corrected.

The viscount seemed to look straight through

her. "Do I? I wonder. It's been three months now and not a word. It makes one wonder."

"You must not despair, my lord," said Caroline, taking the book from his hand and setting it on the shelf again. "There, now it shall be just where he left it when he comes looking for it next."

Lord Rosemeade smiled gratefully.

"Of course. You know, between this rain and my hunger, I've been feeling low, indeed. I may not be able to do anything about the rain, but I can remedy the hunger. Shall we?"

"I'm not feeling at all the thing, Livie. I don't think I'll go to the assembly this evening," Caroline said as she sat down on her friend's bed.

"That's good, dear. You look lovely," said Olivia, not even glancing at Caroline as she sat before her mirror dreamily brushing her hair.

Caroline frowned. This was not going as planned. The old Olivia would have been bustling about trying to make her comfortable upon hearing that Caroline was ill.

"I had thought to wear my pink cravat and tie onions in my hair; what do you think?" said Caroline.

"Uh-hmm," mumbled Olivia.

"Or should it be garlic?"

"Fine, dearest. The . . . What are you talking about?" demanded Olivia suddenly.

Caroline fell back on the bed.

Olivia pursed her lips, raised her chin, and waited for the outburst to end.

"I don't see any need to make game of someone's distraction," she said at last, causing Caroline to sit up.

"I beg your pardon, dearest Livie, but I have never known you to be so lost in thought. What's got you so preoccupied?"

"Caroline, if . . . if I tell you, you must promise—"

"Anything," answered Caroline quickly. A glance at the former governess reassured her that Olivia was not on the verge of unburdening some dark secret; no one's eyes could sparkle just so unless it came from an inner glow.

"It's Mr. Farningham," she whispered. "Oh, Caroline, it's like a miracle! Finding each other again! And now . . . now he wishes to marry me—again!"

After saying this much, Olivia sat back waiting for the shower of joy to come, but Caroline looked perplexed.

"Again? What do you mean? Has he asked you before?"

"Asked, been accepted, and become my husband. Caroline, I thought you had guessed. Ferdie Farningham was my husband fourteen years ago for one week. He is that silly boy I told you about!"

"But I . . . Your . . . And now he wants to marry you again?"

Olivia nodded, her face glowing with happiness.

"I'm so happy for you!" exclaimed Caroline.

"Then you're not upset? I told him I had to discuss it with my niece."

"Of course I'm not upset. Not when I can see how the mere prospect has set you aglow," said Caroline. Her words were sincere, but she could not avoid a deep feeling of trepidation. What would become of their school? Of her?

"I told Ferdie that my niece would make her home with us, so you mustn't worry about that. And if you wish, you may finish at White's before we reveal that little secret to him. I know how important that is to you."

"When will you marry?" asked Caroline.

"Ferdie intends to procure a special license. He said the viscount knows a bishop who is presently in Brighton."

"So soon?" said Caroline, sounding rather forlorn.

Olivia sat down beside her former charge and hugged her.

"I've waited fourteen years, love. I see no reason to put it off."

Caroline managed a bright smile. "Of course you must marry at once. I'm delighted for you."

"Thank you, Caroline. Oh, there's the dinner bell. Why, you haven't dressed yet, dear."

"No, as I was telling you a moment ago, I've got the headache and really don't feel up to it tonight."

"Are you certain? You rarely get a headache. Perhaps if you have some dinner . . ."

"I think not, Livie. You know how I am when I

do get one; it quite defeats me. But you go on. I'll be fine after a good night's sleep."

"I hate to leave you here alone."

"Really, Livie, all I require is sleep."

"If you are certain . . . ?" asked Olivia, hoping her own happy revelation hadn't contributed to Caroline's indisposition.

Left with her thoughts, Caroline fought down a sense of loneliness. She had never felt so alone. How would she manage without Olivia?

As soon as the house grew quiet, Caroline dressed hurriedly in her men's clothes, taking care to bind her bosom flat and to slick her curls back as she tied them with the ribbon.

Earlier in the day, she had visited the stables and taken a bridle and saddle from the tack room. These she had buried in a pile of straw. It was fortunate that Morgan's stall was on the far end, away from the grooms' quarters, so she had no difficulty now in leading the mare away from the stables undetected.

She swung into the saddle, glad to be riding astride once again. It was a much more practical arrangement.

And despite the scolding she was certain to receive if the viscount discovered her, she was exhilarated. How alive she felt!

An hour later, she turned the reins over to an obliging postboy and smoothed her hair before entering the assembly room.

There was such a crowd that it seemed to Caroline as though she were looking through a kaleidoscope. She strolled along the outskirts of the dancers trying to look unobtrusive. With a fixed smile she nodded when nodded to, occasionally acknowledging some acquaintance from White's who knew her as Mr. Pennington. Her air was distracted. Her heart was pounding, making the binding she wore feel even tighter. But resolutely she searched for her quarry.

Half an hour later, Caroline marched up to him boldly.

"*Bonsoir, monsieur le comte,*" she said in a voice that was a shade too loud.

Épernon turned, his eyes wide with surprise.

"Good evening, Charles," he replied, a hint of amusement creeping into his voice. "Allow me to introduce to you Miss Andrews and Mr. Quimby. This is my friend, Mr. Pennington."

Caroline exchanged greetings with impatience. His curiosity piqued, the comte quickly excused himself, taking Caroline with him.

"Now, my impatient friend, though I am flattered, I must admit to being intrigued by your eagerness to be in my company. It is not usually so."

"I have my reasons," she hissed.

He stiffened, curling his lip for an instant. "Have a care, *mon ami*. If you wish to converse here, you must appear to be enjoying it."

Chagrined, she complied. The comte took her arm and began to stroll.

"And now, Caroline, let me tell you what I require of you tonight. There are two young officers here. One is the brother of Willie Needham. I believe you are acquainted with him from White's?" Caroline nodded. "Good. I want you to mingle with them; you will find them in one of the anterooms. Listen and learn what you can from the officers. Understand?"

Caroline nodded miserably before she recalled her own mission.

"I want your help in return," she said with force.

"My help?"

"Yes, but not for me. For the viscount." And for Rosemeade, Caroline determined, she would report accurately anything she learned.

The comte looked around quickly.

"Why should Rosemeade need my help? What have you told him?" he whispered.

"Told him? Nothing! He knows nothing of this."

The comte relaxed once again. "What is it you wish, *mon ami?*"

"I want to know what has become of the viscount's brother."

"Garrett Wyndridge."

Caroline nodded, feeling no surprise that the comte should know about the viscount's family.

"He's in the army, Second Division. He's not been heard from in three months."

"Interesting. But what could I do?" asked the comte.

"The viscount thinks he was sent on a mission of some sort. He had been a special courier before to the allied forces in Prussia. He speaks Prussian and French fluently. I thought, with your influence in France, you might be able to learn if he has been captured."

"*Eh bien*, it is possible. But tell me, why should I do this for you?"

"I . . . I shall go on giving you information."

"But you will do that anyway." He looked her over from head to toe. "We will find some other use for you, my dear. Yes, some other use." Caroline shivered. "Meet me in five days at the west end of the viscount's estate. Come alone."

With this, the comte turned and disappeared into the crowd, leaving Caroline standing like a statue, her heart flip-flopping, her knees almost trembling. But she was determined to carry out Épernon's instructions. After all the viscount had done for her, it was the least she could do in return.

"Glad to see you've recovered, *Mr.* Pennington," said the viscount smoothly, smiling at a passing acquaintance. Caroline's heart jumped into her throat at his voice, and she was unable to utter a syllable. She smiled up at him, hoping to hide her dismay at his untimely appearance.

Trying another tack, Rosemeade commented, "I see our friend the comte is in Brighton."

Caroline shuddered. The viscount regarded her closely. He lowered his voice. His tone invited her confidence, but she chose to remain silent.

"Why do you continue to talk to the man if he repulses you so?"

"Repulses me?" queried Caroline. "You misunderstand, my lord. I merely have a chill."

The viscount glared at her and then walked

away in disgust. Blocking this worry from her mind, Caroline set out to find Mr. Needham, all the while dodging Miss Stanton and the others from Rosemeade. She had to fulfill her mission for the comte or he would refuse to tell her anything about Garrett.

Caroline discovered Willie Needham as he was entering a small side room. He greeted her with more enthusiasm than their nodding acquaintance warranted, slapping her on the back and offering her his flask. She accepted it gratefully; the harsh liquid burned her throat and sharpened her dulled senses.

"Thank you, Mr. Needham."

"M'pleasure, Pennington," said Mr. Needham, his words slurred. Crooking a finger at Caroline, he hooked arms with her and whispered, "Come on in, Penning . . . ington. We've got a little game going. Wanna sit in?"

"I don't . . . By Jove, I believe I shall!" said Caroline. "Though I've not much money," she added.

"No matter, jus' a frien'ly game. None of us are too plump in the pocket."

Caroline was soon seated at the card table along with a pair of red-coated junior officers and two other young men. Each had his money before him and his flask at hand. She looked at their faces, recognizing the two civilians as young men who had entered the club with their fathers a time or two. Willie Needham introduced the officers as his brother and a friend.

They welcomed her cordially, and she deduced that their flasks were already close to empty.

Caroline had learned her lesson, however, and only pretended to share her companions' spirits. She could not afford to become befuddled and lose all her money or speak too freely, but she did laugh at their ribald jokes, even throwing in a remark or two of her own. All the while, she listened to every word the officers uttered, but nothing military was touched upon.

"Ferdie, you escort the ladies home," said Rosemeade. "I've got to speak to someone."

His voice showed his irritation, and Olivia put a hand on his sleeve, drawing him a little away from the others.

"My lord, I saw the comte here. You don't suppose . . ."

He patted her hand, smiling once again. "No, I don't suppose. I wanted to speak to a friend about dining with us soon."

Relieved, Olivia left. The viscount turned, and his face became grim. He hadn't wanted to lie to Olivia, but there was no reason to worry her. He would find his hoydenish young guest and bring her home himself.

He scanned the ballroom, then began opening doors and peering inside dimly lit rooms. After interrupting an entwined couple in one of these, he was about to give up, when he heard raucous laughter escaping from the next room.

Shaking his head at the scene inside, he strode across to the chair on which Caroline was lounging; her cravat had been loosened, her hair was slipping from its unfashionable ribbon, and her grin was decidedly silly. Fortunately, her cohorts appeared in even worse shape.

"Come along, Charles. It's time to go home."

"Hullo, Robert. Let me presen' my frien's."

"No need. I've met them before. Servant, gentlemen. Now, let's go."

They stepped out into the cool night breeze. Caroline took a deep breath, glad to be herself again. But the viscount's anger was tangible, and she felt unequal to the coming scold. She grabbed hold of the viscount's arm, feigning intoxication. His curricle was brought around just then; the viscount swung her into his arms and placed her none too gently on the seat of his curricle. Climbing in himself, he nodded to his tiger, who released the horses' heads.

"Peter, you've seen nothing, you understand?"

The little tiger spat and crossed his heart. "Course not, m'lord."

"Good, now find our guest's mare and ride her home."

"Very good, m'lord."

If Caroline had been wise, she would have remained "asleep." As it was, the jostling movements of the phaeton caused her to lift her head from the viscount's shoulder.

At once, in succinct, biting terms, he began to catalogue her iniquities.

"So! Awake, are you?"

"Robert, I'm sorry."

"Sorry? Good God! Is that all you can say after all this? Nothing we agreed upon—nothing—has stopped you! Have you no sense of decency? Of honor?"

He pulled the horses to a plunging stop, an action that would normally have been inconceivable to him.

"But, Robert," she moaned.

He steeled himself against her pitiful tones.

"You dress up like a man, you go to an assembly—of all places—and you meet with that mountebank Épernon. Have you no discipline?" he thundered.

But Caroline was scrambling out of the carriage; she stumbled away, with the viscount hot on her heels. He grabbed her shoulders and spun her around.

"Oh, no, my girl, you'll not get away as easy as—"

"Robert, leave me alone! You've no right to censure my behavior!" Tears of frustration filled her eyes.

It was a contrite viscount who ushered her back to the phaeton. He settled her as best he could before driving home. Caroline fell asleep at once.

Pulling up by the side entrance to the house, the viscount didn't bother to wake her. He lifted her and carried her past Sanders, who maintained his impassive expression. The bedroom door slammed against the wall as Rosemeade pushed it open; she never stirred.

He dumped Caroline on the bed without ceremony and proceeded to remove her cravat. Shaking his head at the amateur folds and ties, he pulled it from around her neck. She moaned, but didn't wake; the excitement of the evening had been replaced by exhaustion. Muttering under his breath, the viscount flipped her back over and began pulling off her boots.

"Robert?"

"Yes, brat?"

"Am I forgiven?" she asked.

"For the moment."

He removed the hopeless ribbon from her hair and pulled the covers up under her chin.

"Go to sleep."

"Kiss me good night first," murmured Caroline, unwilling to let him go. If he thought her bold, so be it.

Rosemeade peered down at her in the dim light, trying to read her expression. Later he would regret it, but for now he would forget her innocence, her naïvete, and treat her as a woman.

He sat down and pulled her into his rough embrace. Caroline put her arms around his neck and pressed her lips to his.

He pulled away from her, smiling. But her pouting lips beckoned.

A lesser man would not have hesitated. But to Robert Wyndridge, Viscount Rosemeade, honor was not a mere word, it was the very fiber of his life.

Caroline could read the indecision in his eyes.

"Robert," she whispered.

He tightened his arms around her. Lifting her onto his lap, he could feel his desire growing, but he felt powerless to stop. Caroline's sweet kisses intrigued him, teased him; she lacked expertise, but she made up for it in passion.

It was she that made the viscount recall his surroundings, his circumstances. Slowly, his mind regained control, and he realized in horror that he was seducing his houseguest, a maiden whose innocence he could not deny. For though she was passionate, her lack of skill at lovemaking was undeniable. A virgin, without a doubt.

This thought brought him up short, and he staggered to his feet. Caroline whimpered.

"I'm sorry, Caroline. I . . . I forgot myself. I hope you can forgive me," he said.

Deprived of his touch, his kisses, Caroline was engulfed in misery. She felt no shame, only sorrow that he had withdrawn.

But she managed a strangled reply. "I was at fault, too. You are already forgiven."

Still, he stood staring, torn between practicality and emotion. He had escaped any greater folly. Why was he not relieved?

Her voice ragged, Caroline said desperately, "Leave me alone, Robert. Just leave me alone."

He turned on his heel and fled.

Sleep escaped the viscount that night. And as the hours passed, a slow anger grew within him. As is often the case with a proud man, he focused on the wrongs done to him and not on his own transgressions. By morning, he was blameless, and she was a conniving female, one he had unselfishly befriended, who had turned on him.

To justify himself, he reviewed her misdeeds one by one: deceit, disobedience, drunkenness. Seduction, or near seduction, he added, trying to forget the sweet taste of her lips.

Very well, he resolved as the sky turned to gray, he would set her straight. The seed of a plan forming in his mind sprang to life. Yes, he decided, it would serve her right.

Hurriedly, he dressed himself and sent a message to the stables.

First thing in the morning Caroline was downstairs. Her gait was hesitant; she took short steps, almost tiptoeing as she crossed the foyer.

With Épernon in town, she would need to be able to come and go in her guise as Charles Pennington. With this in mind, she hoped to secure a regular saddle, hiding it in the woods.

"Good morning, miss," said Sanders.

After a quick intake of breath at being caught, she managed to return his salutation. The viscount looked out of the breakfast parlor.

"Excellent, Caroline. I was about to have someone roust you!" boomed Rosemeade. "Come along. This morning is much too fine to miss. I've had some fishing gear and a light snack packed. I thought we'd ride to my stock pond. Have you ever fished?"

"Fished, my lord?" said Caroline blankly.

"Yes, I thought Cook might appreciate some fresh trout. Here we are. Mount up."

Gritting her teeth, Caroline mounted onto Morgan's back, hooking her right leg around the upright pommel. The mare twisted her head around to view her rider.

"The man's insane," she told the mare. "Easy, girl, you're carrying fragile cargo this morning." The horse seemed to understand, for she moved off at a smooth walk.

The viscount, not wishing to carry his revenge too far, rode alongside quietly. The estate's fishing pond was not far, and they soon pulled up and dismounted.

The sunlight filtering through the trees glinted silver on the water. Water lilies floated lazily at one end of the pond. The bank was covered with inviting green grass.

Caroline sat down with her knees drawn up; resting her elbows on them, she stifled a yawn. So much for rising early to stash a saddle in the woods. First she had lain awake half the night remembering his kiss; and now this.

"Let's go for a swim!" said Rosemeade, the wicked gleam in his eyes lost to Caroline.

"My lord, I don't wish to be disrespectful, but I'm going to stay right here, in this spot, on this nice, restful grass. I do not make a practice of swimming with gentlemen, but you may do as you please!"

"Tch, tch, how unpleasant we are this morning. I wonder why."

Peering up to tell him what he could do with his wondering, Caroline watched the viscount's coat drop to the ground. She peeked to see him sit down and begin baiting his hook.

"Sure you won't join me?" asked the viscount, throwing his line in the water.

"I'm quite certain," she answered.

Resolutely, she lay back and shut her eyes, and wished she could shut out her misery as easily. Would there always be this deception between them?

"Caroline, Caroline," said the viscount, gently shaking her by the shoulders.

"Wh-what is it?"

"Wake up, child. We need to be getting home," he whispered. Watching her sleep, curled up like a little child, had made him forget his plans for reprisal. He felt embarrassed that his temper had led him to believe so ill of her.

"Home? Oh, the fish."

"I've made a nice catch; you needn't worry about it," said the viscount.

"Already?" asked Caroline, blinking her eyes a few times and taking in the fact that the viscount had replaced his coat; once again, he was the proper host. Fleeting disappointment gripped her; she had wasted this opportunity to have Robert to herself.

"Feeling better?" asked his lordship.

"Much better, my lord. Thank you for letting me sleep," said Caroline humbly.

"Come along. Here's Morgan. I'll give you a leg up."

As their horses sauntered away from the pond,

Rosemeade forced himself to say, "Caroline, I hope you've learned something from all this."

"I have, Robert. Don't worry. If I should ever decide to disobey you again, I shall take care that you don't discover me."

"If I find out about it, I shall thrash you to within an inch of your life, young lady!"

"Just as I said; you shan't find out about it," she said with a laugh.

"I had hoped you'd learned something, Caroline."

"Is that what this morning's escapade was all about? Trying to teach me a lesson?"

"That's about it," admitted the viscount, wondering that he had planned to feel a sense of triumph at the success of this scheme.

"I shall remember this, my lord. I shall remember."

The small wedding planned by Miss Stanton and Mr. Farningham grew somewhat in the four days that followed. By the morning of the ceremony, potted plants and cut flowers filled every room. No fewer than two dozen people had pledged themselves to attend when Lady Hensley "accidentally" let slip the news of the happy event.

The viscount finally dragged his friend to the stables, hoping to distract him for a while. Lady Lietchfield and Lady Hensley took over Olivia, helping her to dress in the peach-colored organdy silk that the viscount had insisted on purchasing for her. Lady Hensley had only mentioned it to him, and he had put Olivia in his carriage and taken her to the dressmaker himself.

The clocks chimed the three-quarter hour as Olivia received the approving nod of Lady Hensley. The older woman wiped away a sentimental tear.

"Come along, Mama. We must find our places," said Lady Lietchfield.

"You look lovely, my dear," repeated Lady Hensley before she hurried away.

"Indeed, dearest Livie, you look radiant," said Caroline, who had been watching the proceedings.

"And you look so beautiful, Caroline, you could be the bride." Olivia giggled.

Laughing too, Caroline strode forward to hug her dearest friend.

Close to tears, Olivia pulled back and, using her best governess tone, said, "Now, you'll be fine here so long as Lady Hensley and Augusta remain. But if they should leave before the week is out, you must return to London, or Cambridge. We'll only be at Robert's hunting lodge for one week, then we'll return to London. You may meet us there."

"I know, Livie. Don't worry about me. I'll be fine."

They heard the clock strike eleven.

"It's time."

Olivia nodded and placed her hand in Caroline's to walk downstairs.

* * *

"It was a beautiful ceremony," pronounced Lady Hensley as they sat down at the wedding breakfast.

"Just the same as countless others I've seen," observed a cynical Sir Kendall.

"You men are all alike, sir," admonished Lady Hensley. "No romance in your souls."

The old, gray-haired squire leaned forward and gave a broad wink. "We've romance enough, my lady. Just of a different sort."

She laughed and tapped his arm with her fan. "You are a saucy one!"

"A toast to the happy couple." All eyes traveled from the viscount to Ferdie and Olivia, and glasses were raised. "May you enjoy a long and happy life together."

After the final course was served, Olivia rose and was accompanied upstairs by Lady Hensley, Augusta, and the Countess of Aberley. Ferdie soon retreated to his own chamber to dress for the first leg of their journey to Leicestershire.

Feeling unequal to the task of helping, Caroline found refuge in the library until it was time to send off the newlyweds. She hurried down the long corridor to the side entrance, where the guests waited, armed with rice. Stationed just inside with the viscount, Caroline fixed a smile on her face and concentrated on keeping the tears at bay.

"Here they come," said someone.

The new Mrs. Farningham stopped in front of

the viscount. "Thank you, my lord, for everything."

After kissing her cheek, he said, "I can't think when anything has given me more pleasure." Then, without another word, he grasped Ferdie's hand and moved out the door, leaving Caroline alone with the newlyweds.

"I'll take care of her, Miss Pennington."

"I know, Ferdie," said Caroline, still managing to smile. "Good-bye, Aunt Olivia. Have a wonderful trip."

"Thank you, Caroline. Now, you take care," said Mrs. Farningham, also holding back tears through great effort. Hugging her niece once, she pulled away and was quickly lost among the shower of rice and laughing well-wishers.

Caroline turned on her heel. Unable to stop the tears any longer, she hurried to her chamber. Here, she quickly changed to breeches and boots, covering the breeches with a voluminous riding skirt. Slipping down the servants' staircase, she was soon striding toward the stables. She stood in the shadows while Henry placed a sidesaddle on Morgan. She would soon exchange it for the saddle in the woods. Then, before anyone could detect her, she was away.

Passing through a field at a mild canter, Caroline looked ahead to see a familiar figure by the fence fifty yards in front of her. She pulled the mare up, momentarily unable to force herself to ride closer.

Gustave Thibault waved her forward, and she picked up the reins again. Aware of her rider's unease, the little mare pranced daintily. Being constrained to concentrate on keeping her seat, Caroline managed to present a detached countenance to Thibault.

"Allons-y," growled the Frenchman, motioning toward the open gate. Without a word, Caroline followed.

They rode in silence for a mile or so before reaching a deserted hut. The comte appeared in the doorway at their approach.

"Bonjour, mon ami. I have news for you."

"I assumed as much when I encountered your henchman. That is why I am here," said Caroline.

The comte signaled for her to come sit on the stone bench by the door.

"I have discovered that your viscount's brother is a prisoner."

Caroline gasped.

"Eh bien, it is not so bad. He was mistaken for a Prussian soldier instead of being shot for the spy he is. Therefore, his life is in no danger, unless, of course, someone informs the commander." Pausing, he let the threat hang in the air.

"Where is he being held?" asked Caroline.

"He is among the prisoners who are building a canal that will connect the rivers Saône and Doubs, just outside Dijon."

"Is there any way to free him?" asked Caroline.

"There is a hope, but it will require a great deal of courage. I have a name . . ."

"Well, what is it?" demanded Caroline.

"So impatient, eh, my little one?" said the comte, covering her knee with his long fingers.

Caroline glared at him, removing his hand from her knee. The comte laughed heartily at this, amused by her bravado.

"Now, my sweet Caroline, first you must give the information you gathered."

She turned pale. "They didn't talk about their units or anything, I swear. I stayed and stayed, but they never broached the topic at all."

His eyes narrowed. Caroline waited for the blow, but none came.

"No matter now. There will be others."

"So you'll give me the name of the man who can free the viscount's brother?"

"He will help, at least. His name is Thomas Sinclair. He is an Englishman of dubious reputation and inexplicable wealth. In this area, that usually means smuggling," he explained.

"You and the viscount must go just outside Brighton; on the road to Eastbourne is a small tavern called the Black Sand. Ask for Sinclair there."

"Thank you, *monsieur*," said Caroline, rising and walking away.

"*Un moment*, Caroline," said Épernon. The coldness in his voice made her turn to face him. "There is more. We had a bargain, you will remember."

She swallowed hard.

"I have arranged for the viscount's brother to be brought to the coast near Normandy. You and the viscount will go together. Sinclair will bring you across. He is only one of an entire network of smugglers, thieves, traitors, and spies. I want them all. You will return to England with a list of names, places, and so forth."

"No! I can't!".

"And when you return, you will be of no further use to me." He waited a moment before adding in a quiet undertone, "The alternative would be so unpleasant—for you, for the brother, and for your precious viscount."

The comte had risen and advanced toward her. Under his hard stare, Caroline wavered, then nodded her acquiescence.

"I wondered where you'd gone, Charles. Servant, Épernon."

Caroline whirled around at the viscount's voice. Even Épernon paled as he gazed up into the viscount's steely eyes.

"Of course, I'd no idea my grounds were inhabited by such fascinating guests."

"My lord," began the comte, recovering his composure.

"Robert, I asked Épernon to meet me here when he had news," said Caroline.

Swinging down from the saddle, Rosemeade said coolly, "News? Now, what news might that be?"

"Of your brother, Garrett, *monsieur*," said Épernon, noting the spark of interest in the viscount's eyes.

"What could you possibly know of Garrett?"

"Please, Robert. I asked the comte to help. I

thought he might be able to obtain some word. And he has!" Her pleading tone was not wasted on the viscount. He turned to her.

Kindly, he said, "Go home, Charles. I appreciate your efforts, but let me talk to Épernon alone."

"Yes, my lord," she obeyed, and allowed him to throw her into the saddle. She rode off without another word.

Chapter Nine

Caroline settled in the library to wait for the viscount's return. She pulled a copy of Weatherby's *Introduction to a General Stud Book*, telling herself she must learn more about horses if she wanted to converse intelligently with Ferdie. But even at the best of times, the book would have been a bore. After only a few minutes, Caroline laid it aside, admitting her case was hopeless.

One moment she was wishing the viscount would enter, tell her Épernon had been lying and that they were staying at Rosemeade. The next, she found herself hoping she would be able to help his lordship rescue his brother.

It was dusk before she heard his footstep at the door; Caroline sat up stiffly and spread her skirts down around her ankles. She expected a terrible scold.

Instead, the viscount entered and sat down across from her, staring into her eyes as though trying to read there the answer to some complex problem.

Prompting him, Caroline asked, "My lord, what did you decide?"

He continued to gaze at her in that probing manner.

"Robert?"

"I leave tomorrow night."

"But what about me? Épernon said I should go, too."

"So he informed me. I refused."

"But how will you manage? You've told me you don't speak the language very well."

"I shall manage. Good God, Caroline! How could you think I would allow it? This is not some great lark; this is life or death! Dressing as a boy and working at White's every day was foolish, but the only damage, if you'd been discovered, would have been to your reputation. And mine. But this!" Then he stood up and began pacing back and forth. At last, he settled behind the large oak desk that dominated the far end of the room.

Caroline crossed to stand before him. With his fingertips together, he peered at her over the little steeple. She smiled, recalling the first interview she endured at the hands of the Viscount Rosemeade. How cold she had thought him then!

The viscount misunderstood her smile.

"You still don't comprehend the gravity of the situation, do you? How do you suppose Épernon located my brother? How can he arrange Garrett's escape? And why? I don't trust the man."

Caroline was seized by a sudden fear for him.

"Then don't go, Robert! If I've led you into a trap, I would never forgive myself!"

He stood up and circled the desk quickly with his long strides. Taking her trembling form in a brotherly embrace, he attempted to reassure her, for the decision had already been made. He had to try!

"Come now, child. I'm sure my suspicions are unfounded. After all, Épernon didn't have to put himself out over this. Obviously, I have simply misjudged him in the past. Don't worry; everything will go according to plan. I must tell you one thing: I was relieved Épernon hadn't discovered your secret. If he knew you for a female . . ."

Caroline looked up expectantly, debating on whether or not to admit the truth.

But Rosemeade only smiled and said, "When all is said and done, he is a Frenchman."

After taking a deep breath, he became the concerned host once more.

"Where are the ladies?"

"They're dining with the Weatherreds and attending the card party there. I told them you had urgent business matters to finish."

"Good girl! I'm in no mood for pleasantries. But I do intend to stay awake all night so I can sleep during the day tomorrow. How about backgammon?"

"I accept," she said, delighted to have an evening alone with "her" viscount.

They heard the ladies return, but by unspoken consent, they remained hidden away in the library. Tiring of backgammon, they switched to piquet and then to chess. The viscount made several halfhearted attempts to send Caroline to her bed, but he accepted her disavowal of fatigue quickly enough; he felt the need of some company to occupy his thoughts.

As the gray fingers of dawn spread across the sky, they exchanged a weary "Good night" and sought their beds.

Caroline slept until afternoon. When she awoke, she dressed in her riding habit and hurried to the stables. Soon she was speeding across the estate to the small hut where she had met the comte the previous day. As she had guessed, he was there waiting.

"Welcome, my dear. I thought you might show up, but I was growing weary with the wait. How lovely you look in your riding habit."

Ignoring the compliment, she said curtly, "You knew I needed to talk to you. The viscount still refuses to take me with him."

"Then he and his brother will die. He is an exceedingly foolish man," the comte murmured as he continued to pare his nails.

"But why? I couldn't protect them!"

He touched her cheek, causing Caroline to shiver in revulsion.

"You are wrong, *ma chérie*. As I told you before, you have your own mission. Unless you do your part, I can make no guarantee as to the safety of this endeavor."

"So you would let them be killed if I don't bring you back those names."

"Undoubtedly."

Caroline took a deep breath, torn between obeying the viscount or the comte. With Épernon's snakelike eyes peering at her, she made her decision.

"I'll need clothes so I can sneak on board the ship without the viscount's knowledge."

"Robert, I don't wish to be a bore, dearest, but exactly why did you invite me to Rosemeade?" asked Lady Lietchfield as they strolled arm in arm through the formal gardens.

"To enjoy the company of yourself and your lovely mother."

But her ladyship was in no mood for evasion.

"Robert, we both know you've spent more time with Caroline Pennington than with me."

"Be reasonable, Augusta."

She shook her head. "I'm returning to London in the morning." If Augusta had hoped he would protest, she was disappointed.

"Perhaps it would be for the best, my dear," said Rosemeade.

Augusta lifted her china blue eyes and studied

his face. Standing on tiptoe, she delivered a chaste kiss to his cheek.

"Miss Pennington is a fortunate girl," she said before returning to the house.

Robert watched her retreat absentmindedly. How wrong Augusta was, he thought. But he frowned impatiently as a flood of relief washed over him. With Augusta gone, things would be simplified.

Things? he demanded. Suddenly, he turned on his heel, heading for the stables. An invigorating gallop would soon blow the cobwebs from his mind. His thoughts should be on the upcoming journey, not on tiresome females.

"My lord?" said Caroline by way of greeting when he almost walked into her on the path.

"Oh, Caroline. Good, I need to talk to you."

"Yes, my lord?" she asked, hoping beyond hope he had changed his mind about her going to France. She so hated to deceive him!

"Augusta and her mother are leaving for London in the morning. I'll ask them to take you with them."

"No!" she cried.

"Be reasonable, girl," Rosemeade insisted, running his fingers through his hair at the thought of another confrontation with a hysterical female.

"You can't ask it of me, Robert," she pleaded, her large brown eyes filling with tears. "You must let me stay until you return; the wait will be unbearable as it is."

He touched her cheek, his thumb blotting away the lone tear that had fallen.

"Very well, my dear, you may stay. But as soon as I get back, it's off to Olivia and Ferdie with you! Understood?"

Caroline nodded, trying not to contemplate the extent of his anger when she stowed away on the smugglers' boat. There would be no tender touches then.

The viscount turned back toward the house, offering her his arm. "Will you join me in a drink? I think Sanders can find some lemonade."

As darkness settled in, two figures in rough homespun made their separate ways to the Black Sand. The viscount arrived first; he went directly to a door at the rear of the tavern and entered a small storeroom.

Caroline slipped inside a moment later. Before her eyes became adjusted to the light, a large hand grabbed her shoulder, squeezing it with brutal force.

"Jes' where d'ye think yer going, laddie?"

Caroline was spun around to face three menacing pairs of eyes glaring at her suspiciously.

"Nowhere, I—" she squeaked as the one holding her tightened his grip.

"The boy's with me," the viscount interrupted, brandishing a heavy pistol.

"Yer sure, guvner?"

"You doubt my word?" he asked, turning the muzzle of the gun toward the speaker. The three men backed away. "Come on, boy, quit dawdling," said Rosemeade, grabbing Caroline and shoving her behind him.

Satisfied, the three men withdrew.

"Robert," whispered Caroline.

"Not a word, or I'll throw you back to those cutthroats," he growled.

Meekly, she obeyed, trying to appear invisible.

From his conversation with Sinclair the day before, the viscount knew to pull the heavy sea locker upward and climb down the ladder hidden beneath it. When Caroline was through, he lighted one of the lanterns hanging by the ladder and pulled the trapdoor back into place.

They soon reached firm ground and began walking the damp corridor that led to the beach. After ten minutes, the low ceiling gave way to a higher one, and the viscount stretched gratefully.

Whispering, he said, "Back there, the passage was mostly man-made. This is part of a cave that leads to the beach. At high tide, the mouth of the cavern is probably underwater."

"It's all like a very bad novel. I expect to see the evil count soon," commented Caroline. The viscount shot her a quizzical look but made no reply.

When they reached the beach, Caroline saw men scurrying everywhere. But what struck her was the silence. The only noise rose from the sea rushing up on the shore. The men worked in silence, ignoring them.

The viscount put his hand out to stop her, then walked forward to speak in a low voice to one of the smugglers. He signaled, and she hurried to his side. They were stowed away like the rest of the cargo on the fishing boat.

Suddenly, everyone leaped aboard; and Caroline peeked to see that they were out in the water, the light sail taking them away from shore. She settled back again, her shoulders touching the viscount's. He seemed to be asleep, but Caroline could sense his tension and she longed to comfort him.

This thought made her grin. What would these rough sailors do if they saw a young man giving the viscount comfort? She almost laughed outright. And Robert? What would he think?

Her smile vanished at this sobering thought. She could imagine what he would say if he discovered she had agreed to spy for the comte. Or worse, he wouldn't speak at all; he would only turn away in disgust.

Though the moon had begun to rise, none of the crew noticed the silent tears that coursed down the cheeks of their young passenger.

The activity onboard became hurried once more; each man knew his job and performed it in silence. An anchor was dropped, and Caroline looked toward shore to see four dinghies coming toward them in the dim moonlight. She turned to wake the viscount, but he was awake already and at her side. He whispered and slipped something into her pocket. She realized it was a pistol.

The man she assumed was Sinclair said in a gruff tone, "Yer guide's waitin' onshore. Remember, you have until dark tomorrow. If you're not here we'll sail without you."

Minutes later, they reached the shore. So this is France, thought Caroline. She noticed that the viscount held his hand on his own pistol. It was clear he expected trouble. She slipped her own hand into her coat pocket and felt the heavy gun.

All day long they waited. The only sound was of quiet waves lapping against the shore.

It was dusk when a stout figure spoke to them from the shadows. *"Monsieur,* I have been waiting for you," he said.

"Very good, sir. Now, where is my brother?" the viscount answered in his best schoolroom French.

The man indicated a lifeless figure lying at his feet on the sand.

The viscount strode forward, kneeling on one knee. "Garrett," he said simply. "It is I."

The man sat up. "Robert! You must leave at once," he shouted. "This is a trap!"

At that moment a hand closed over her mouth. Caroline looked up to see the hulking figure of Gustave Thibault. She would have fainted, but the sudden sound of the comte's voice shocked her so, her heart began to beat faster.

"Don't bother to shoot," the comte said. "Gustave has his orders, regardless."

"Orders from whom? Your emperor?" said Robert.

"Ah, no, *cher* Rosemeade. The orders are from me. I have arranged all this, and it is I who will be rewarded by Bonaparte. Though I must thank our dear Charles, who has been very industrious in furthering my cause. I daresay I couldn't have managed without you. And now, you will please drop you weapons."

Caroline, her hand still in her coat, made no attempt to comply, but she managed to turn the pistol so that it pointed, she prayed, at Thibault's generous stomach. The viscount dropped his gun. She knew the rest was up to her.

Shutting her eyes tightly, she gripped the pistol inside her pocket and gently squeezed the trigger as she had been instructed.

The report of the gun was deafening, and she screamed despite herself. Thibault dropped his hand, the knife falling to the sand as he clutched the blackened hole in his coat before stumbling backward.

Caroline froze, unable to take her eyes from the prostrate Thibault. The comte turned his gun on her, oblivious to all else in his desire for revenge. Taking careful aim, he, too, squeezed the trigger, but a split second before he did, another shot rang out.

Épernon staggered; his shot missed its target, only hitting Caroline's shoulder and knocking her to the sand.

"Charles, are you hit?" the viscount yelled as he raced to her side, still waving his weapon.

The dying comte watched this scene with contempt. "All Englishmen are fools. He still doesn't understand; doesn't understand at all," he said weakly, his laugh choked in a gurgle of blood.

Chapter Ten

Garrett Wyndridge was left puzzled by the comte's cryptic words. Then he moved to his brother's side and learned the injured man was Rosemeade's clerk.

"How is he? Is he badly hurt?"

The viscount shook his head. "Just fainted. Wait for us at the shore and watch for our dinghy," he ordered.

Garrett complied, leaving his brother alone with his clerk. Reaching inside the heavy coat to staunch the blood had unnerved the viscount. Now he finished unbuttoning the rough shirt and purposefully removed his knife to cut through the binding around Caroline's chest. She sighed and opened her eyes.

"Robert," she whispered.

"Quiet!" he growled. "I don't know what you've been to Épernon, but you did save my life, and I'll get you back to England, alive. After that, you can leave, go anywhere you please. I don't care."

"But, Robert, I—"

"No explanations, please," he said sarcastically as he stuffed the binding against her wound. She winced, but his anger was such that he didn't care.

"I don't want to know why or how. If you were working for Épernon, you're out of a job, but that's not my concern. Just keep your mouth closed."

In her pain and misery, Caroline could do nothing else.

After wrapping the wound tightly and rebuttoning her shirt, the viscount pronounced her ready and stood up, striding away from her without a backward glance. Garrett, who had been watching, came over and sat down on the sand beside her.

"Need anything? Wine?"

"No." She sniffed.

"How well do you know my brother?"

She just shook her head, afraid to speak lest she cry out in her desolation.

"Hmm. That well, eh?" He smiled at her with those same gray eyes. "Then you already know he has a frightful temper."

He studied her carefully for a moment.

"Yes, I see signs that you've experienced it firsthand. Then you should also know he doesn't mean the half of it."

"Not this time," she moaned.

"Don't be an ass, Pennington! Mark my words; he'll forget."

She managed what she hoped was a brave smile, but inside she could not rid herself of Robert's look of disbelief and horror. She folded her arms across her chest, ignoring the stab of pain in her shoulder.

"Get the light," called the viscount from where he stood gazing out at the Channel. Garrett produced a shuttered lantern, which they uncovered three times.

"This is it. Get our things," he ordered as the dinghy touched the beach.

"No cargo tonight, exceptin' you, sir."

The viscount extended his hand and said gratefully, "I'm glad you made it, Sinclair."

Once again they huddled together in the boat, but Caroline thought she had never been more miserable than she was during that crossing. Her leg and hip touched the viscount's, but she could take no comfort in this. Her shoulder throbbed horribly, and the thought of the ball still lodged inside her was making her nauseous. Garrett found an old sail with which to cushion her head and tried to make her comfortable, but so deep in misery was she that she forgot to thank him.

Caroline was in a semiconscious state by the time they landed in a small cove. She knew when they were carrying her off the boat, but she could neither stop nor aid them. She was barely aware of the rough journey and only realized they had reached Rosemeade when she heard the viscount call for a surgeon as he carried her up the steps.

As he placed Caroline on her bed, Rosemeade could not help but remember the night—was it only a week ago?—he had carried Caroline up to her bed. To think he had almost been seduced by this traitor.

Garrett followed him into the room and started to remove Caroline's boots.

"I'll do that," his brother snapped. Then, looking up at Garrett, he sighed wearily. "Sorry, I'm exhausted. You go to bed, Garrett. I'll tend to Charles myself."

With this unquestionable dismissal, his lordship turned to Sanders, who hovered by the door.

"See to it that Mr. Garrett gets a bath and a hot rum punch before he gets to bed. We don't want you getting sick, Garrett."

"Very good, my lord. And for yourself?"

"Send me some breakfast and a big pot of coffee. Oh, and have Rivers get me a change of clothes and hot water."

"Certainly, my lord," said Sanders, and he closed the door behind him.

Alone with Caroline, he began to strip off her clothes in a very businesslike manner. He cleansed the wound and bound it again, working dispassionately. Then he proceeded to bathe her from head to toe. The viscount rummaged through the dresser and produced a nightgown. Putting this on the unconscious Caroline was quite an operation; it was difficult to judge who grunted and groaned more, the dresser or the patient.

There was a knock on the door, and the viscount quickly threw the coverlet over her. She looked terribly still and frail, but there was no denying the swell of her breasts inside the soft lawn nightgown.

"Your clothes, my lord," said the viscount's valet, beginning to unfasten his master's rough shirt with obvious distaste.

Rosemeade pushed his hands away. "I'll do this, Rivers. You go on. See where my coffee . . . Ah, here's Sanders now. Thank you, that will be all."

Puzzled yet obedient, the valet and the butler retreated.

The viscount threw off his clothes and bathed as best he could from the washbasin. He pulled on his breeches, shirt, and socks, but decided to forgo boots and cravat. He pulled a chair close to the bed and set his plate and cup on the bedside table.

With a hearty breakfast and two cups of coffee downed, he felt he could handle the day ahead.

Closing his eyes, he tried to block the past twelve hours from his mind, but scenes kept flashing before him like a play with too many acts. Impatiently, he strode to the window and looked down at the rose garden. The fragrance drifting up reminded him of his gentle father, who could always be found among his beloved flowers. His mother had been the one with the temper, and he had always been his mother's son.

Caroline groaned and moved restlessly under the heavy quilt.

"Robert," she wailed in a helpless whine.

"Shh, shh, I'm here," said the viscount as he pushed her back down.

His voice and touch were gentle. Caroline opened her eyes, but the gray eyes staring back were implacable. She shut her eyes quickly, giving in to the black velvet oblivion of exhaustion.

"My lord," said a tall, spare man who was standing beside Garrett at the door.

"Dr. Witherspoon, glad you could get here so soon," said the viscount, striding forward with his hand outstretched. It was obvious from Garrett's expression that he and the doctor had just witnessed the scene, had perhaps even heard Caroline's unmistakably feminine voice.

"You come in, too, Garrett. Before the good doctor sees his patient, I must talk with both of you. Shut the door."

Garrett and Dr. Witherspoon exchanged puzzled glances and entered the room. The viscount hesitated.

"What is it, my lord? I should like to examine Mr. Pennington."

"That is it, precisely. Mr. Pennington is in reality Miss Pennington."

The doctor looked skeptical; Garrett's confusion changed to amusement. He chuckled, then he laughed. Then he laughed louder still and was soon clutching his side, stumbling around trying to keep his balance.

Lord Rosemeade curled his lip in brotherly disdain.

"Captain Wyndridge, would you please take yourself off? Mr. or Miss, I must tend to my patient," said the doctor, removing his black frock coat and rolling up his sleeves.

Garrett managed a nod and headed for the door, but his brother was before him. The viscount caught his arm firmly.

"Not a word of this leaves this room. Do you understand? The servants are to think this is Miss Pennington's brother. The fewer who know, the better."

The viscount shut the door and returned to the bed. The doctor exposed the wound and shook his head.

"The ball is deep, my lord, very deep. It will be quite painful for her while I probe for it. You will hold her arms and be ready to steady her head if I tell you."

"Yes, sir."

The viscount gritted his teeth as the doctor produced a long, curved instrument and began to delve into the open wound, searching for the piece of lead. Caroline moaned and then cried out; he paused for a moment. The viscount held her arms tightly as she moved away from the searing pain.

"I see it!" said the doctor suddenly. He went to work retrieving the ball, and Rosemeade tried to soothe Caroline though it was doubtful she heard him. Her initial scream was cut off abruptly as she slipped into unconsciousness.

As Dr. Witherspoon replaced his instruments and his coat, the viscount sat on the edge of the bed, weak-kneed and exhausted.

"I'll come by this evening, my lord. It's the next three days that must concern us now. If she can make it that long, and with no fever, we're out of the woods."

"Any instructions?" the viscount asked without rising.

"Fluids if she wakes; perhaps a little broth. The essential part is to keep her calm and quiet, so the fever will not develop. Good luck, my lord."

Garrett stepped inside as the doctor exited. He looked completely recovered and even contrite, so the viscount welcomed him.

"I want to apologize, Robert. But you see, I was fooled. I thought she was a boy all along. I never suspected. I suppose that was what Épernon meant."

The viscount sat up.

"Épernon?"

"Yes, just before he died, he said, 'All Englishmen are fools. He still doesn't understand.'"

The viscount's jaw tightened at this, and his gaze grew brittle. Garrett stepped back a pace.

"Robert?" he said.

"So Épernon knew, too; he knew all along," said the viscount.

"What was that?"

His lordship focused on his brother's worried frown, and he said in a normal tone, "Go to bed, Garrett. I'd like for you to spell me this evening."

"Of course, Robert. You may count on me," he said, but as he left, he remained uncertain that his words had been heard. The viscount had already returned to his vigil by the bed.

Evening came, and Dr. Witherspoon announced there was no change. Garrett took his place by the bedside of the unconscious girl. Her breathing was shallow and contained the hint of a whistle as she exhaled.

When the viscount returned after midnight, Caroline still had not moved. He told Garrett quietly that he would stay till breakfast. The captain nodded and went away, leaving his brother to resume his lonely vigil.

With each breath he heard, it seemed as

though someone was shouting at him, "Épernon knew . . . Épernon knew . . ." Finally, he began humming to drown out his thoughts. He carefully chose a mournful tune, "Barbara Allan," which would not lift his flagging spirits.

The next day passed uneventfully. There was no change in the patient. Garrett stayed by the bed throughout the morning and was surprised to see the viscount shortly after one.

"I'll take over now."

"But, Robert, you haven't even been to bed."

"I can sleep here in this chair just as easily as anywhere else. Now run along, little brother."

Dr. Witherspoon arrived just before dinner and pronounced the wound clean and healing. The patient's unconscious state he could not explain, so he went away muttering under his breath and shaking his head in a thoughtful manner.

After seeing the doctor downstairs, Captain Wyndridge returned to stand beside the door and observe, not Caroline but his older brother.

"Garrett, can you not think of anything better to do?" said the viscount after enduring several minutes of this.

"As a matter of fact, brother, yes, I can."

"Then please do it."

"Very well." He walked to the bell rope and gave it a decisive tug. "I'm having a screen and a cot moved into this room, and I intend to sleep here tonight."

"There's no need for that," said the viscount, stifling a yawn.

"Rubbish! Look at yourself in the mirror. In the past week, you've not had a single decent night's sleep, and it shows. I realize you feel responsible for Miss Pennington's condition, but—"

"Ha! I? How may that be? Was it I who set up the scheme with Épernon? Was it I who stowed away on the smugglers' boat? Was it I who stepped in at the wrong time?" As he spoke, the viscount strode up and down the room, gesticulating wildly. "And what's more—"

"Enough, Robert, enough. I didn't say it was your fault, but you're acting as though it is. Why won't you at least go downstairs to dine? I'll sit with Miss Pennington."

His energy and emotions spent, the viscount agreed.

Caroline was dreaming; she was riding, but the ground kept sinking away from her horse's hooves. She tried to make the animal touch the ground, but they kept getting higher and higher. And there was Robert, down on the ground. She called to him, but he ignored her. She called again, but he still refused to look up. She yelled as loudly as she could, repeating his name over and over in a desperate tone.

"Miss Pennington! Miss Pennington! Wake up! You're having a bad dream! Wake up!"

She lifted her heavy eyelids. Blurry, so very blurry. She shut her eyes, then opened them wide, making a great effort to focus on the face peering down at her. Perhaps it's Robert, she thought.

"Robert, forgive me," she whispered. Her vision cleared. With a sob, she said, "Garrett, handsome Garrett."

"I thank you," he said excitedly. "Now, Miss—"

"Caroline, just Caroline."

"Pardon me, I wasn't certain. After all, I was introduced to a Mr. Pennington." Scrutinizing her face as closely as an artist might, he added, "No, you're right. You can't be that Mr. Pennington. You're far too pretty."

She smiled weakly at his sally.

"But here, let me get you some water. Are you hungry?"

She drank the water gratefully but turned away from the broth. Caroline noticed her nightclothes for the first time.

Fingering the soft material, she asked timidly, "How did I get into this?"

Garrett said, keeping his expression steady, "I don't know. You were dressed like that the first time I saw you here."

"But I couldn't have undressed — What I mean is, who . . . ?"

"Robert carried you up all by himself, so I suppose . . ."

Garrett let it hang. If Caroline had not been as white as the pillowcase before, she turned as pale at this news. The viscount had undressed her! This was too much!

The Scandalous Miss

"Please, Garrett, may I see Robert?"

He frowned. "I sent him downstairs for dinner. But if I know Robert, he'll be back in here soon. You just rest till he arrives. That's a good girl."

Garrett extinguished all the candles but three, and with the added incentive of darkness, Caroline slept.

True to his brother's prediction, the viscount appeared soon after dinner. When Garrett told him Caroline had awakened, his eyes hardened, and he started for her bedchamber.

"Robert!" whispered Garrett. "Not now. She's asleep again."

"Again? Very well, then I'll wait. You go on; I'll take the cot."

"That's not why I had it moved in here."

"Nevertheless, I'll use it. Run along like a good boy, Garrett," the viscount ordered. "I'll stay with Caroline."

Some note in his brother's teasing words made Garrett hesitate to leave the weak girl alone with him. But he looked into those inflexible gray eyes and conceded; there had been too many years of obeying that look.

Caroline moaned softly and began to twist in the bed. The viscount was off the cot and by her side at once.

"Livie, Livie," she cried softly.

"Mrs. Farningham is not here, Caroline. I am. It's—"

"Robert?" she said, opening her eyes and remembering where she was. "Robert, how did you get me home? I . . . I don't remember. I've had dreams, and I'm not sure anymore what really happened."

"Home?" he queried, unable to keep the sarcasm from his voice. "I got you back to Rosemeade in a dogcart."

Caroline was very weak, but she knew he was still angry. Though he was not scolding her, his tones were flat, emotionless.

"And you . . . you put me to bed?" she whispered.

With an effort, he said coldly, "Yes, I put you to bed. I couldn't very well ask an abigail to undress Mr. Pennington, could I?"

She winced and shook her head.

"Garrett tells me you claim your name, at least, is really Caroline," said the viscount, unable to hold back his anger. "I had begun to wonder if anything you'd told me was true."

"The only lie was about my sex, Robert, and you were not long deceived in that."

"And I'm supposed to believe that? What kind of fool do you take me for? Oh, I forgot, the worst kind, no doubt. How you and Epernon must have laughed!"

"No! It wasn't like that!"

"Then what was it like, you and the comte?"

"He . . . he knew about me."

"Obviously. Is that why he enjoyed your company? That night you dined at his house, what else did he enjoy?"

"Stop it!" she screamed, rising up on one el-

The Scandalous Miss

bow. "The comte found out; he was blackmailing me, making me give him information I heard at the club."

The viscount dropped into the chair at her bedside, an incredulous look on his face.

"My God! I didn't want to believe what Épernon said on the beach that night. It's worse than I thought. You were spying for him!"

She sobbed with frustration, saying, "It wasn't like that! I never told him anything that was true. But I was frightened!"

Rosemeade extended a hand, wanting to comfort her, but he withdrew it, hardening himself against her pleas. He stood up and walked to the window.

"Why, Caroline? If you'd only come to me, told me what was happening, I would have stopped him."

Tears streamed down her cheeks. "He threatened to kill Livie," she said out loud. And you! she wanted to scream. "I couldn't let that happen."

The viscount took a deep breath. "So what will you do now?" he asked flatly.

"I don't know. I need time. After I finish the library at White's—"

"Finish the . . . ?" interrupted his lordship, rounding on her again. "Have you no shame? How can you think of going back there? Even if you don't care about your own reputation, there are other people to consider! Ferdie, Olivia, myself!"

Caroline drew herself up on her good elbow

again with great effort. Panting, she said disdainfully, "Livie would understand my reasons, and I daresay Ferdie would too. It seems you, my lord, are the only one concerned who is not adult enough to handle a slur on his precious reputation."

As she glared at him, her eyes followed him to the door.

In that terrifying calm voice, he said, "I'll leave your wages with my man. Forget White's library and go home—or anywhere you please, so long as it's away from Rosemeade, away from me. Good-bye."

The door closed.

Caroline fell back on the pillow, ignoring the bolt of pain this caused. It was nothing compared to the emptiness in her heart.

The viscount went straight to his own chamber and began throwing shirts into a valise. Rivers was awakened by the noise and entered the room in alarm, the tails of his nightshirt flapping.

"My lord, my lord, what is it?"

"I'm packing."

"My lord, surely you don't mean to . . ." Seeing his words had no effect on his master, he inquired, "And what is our destination, my lord?"

"My destination, Rivers, is Scotland. I'm going fishing."

"Fishing, my lord," repeated the poor valet.

"Have you become hard of hearing, Rivers?

Fishing in Scotland. I'm leaving first thing in the morning. You stay here. I can look after myself."

"Very good, my lord. If your lordship will allow me, I'll just rearrange these things a little," said the valet.

"Do as you please, Rivers. I'm going to get a little sleep before this night is over. Wake me at five."

"Caroline, how are you today? It's good to see you awake. Where's my brother?"

"Good morning, Garrett," she said weakly.

"Where's Robert?" he repeated. "Already up and about?"

"I . . . I don't know."

Concern clouded Garrett's eyes as he noted that Caroline was no longer pale but looked flushed and bright-eyed. He placed a hand on her forehead; it was dry and warm.

"I'll be back." With this, he left quickly, almost running in his haste to find his brother. He threw open the door to the viscount's bedchamber.

"Rivers, where's my brother?" he demanded.

"In Scotland, sir. At least that is where he is going."

"He's gone to Scotland without so much as a by-your-leave? Who the hell does he think he is?"

Since Garrett's question required no answer, Rivers remained silent.

Producing a pair of letters from his pocket, the valet said, "His lordship left this packet for Mr.

Pennington. Also, he left this note and purse for you, sir. He said it contains his direction."

After a quick perusal of it, Garrett nodded. He returned to Caroline with the letter and the velvet purse, which made an interesting clinking sound as he handed it to her.

"Robert left this for you," he said. "I've no idea what the letter says, but I hope you won't refine too much upon it. He was still quite overset when he wrote it."

She nodded dumbly, then looked up at him, her jaw set and the look in her brown eyes strong and determined.

"I'll leave you now, Caroline. Good night."

"Thank you, Garrett."

He glanced back at her, his hand resting on the cold brass doorknob.

I must get away, she thought miserably as she sank back among the bedclothes.

It was two weeks before Caroline could make good her escape. Later one night, Caroline pulled out her worn valise and carefully folded her shirts, breeches, and cravats, and placed them inside. Impatiently, she dashed a tear from her cheek.

Satisfied she had packed everything she would need, she composed a note to Garrett. Finally, she took up the small bag of coins. The note, still wrapped around it, was written in the viscount's bold hand.

Payment for services rendered.

She tore it up, leaving the pieces on top of the chest. With one decisive movement, she placed the money in her valise and slipped out the door.

The silence of the corridor was eerie, but Caroline squared her shoulders and hurried along the hall and down the servants' stairs. She made her way to the east side of the house, then slipped out the entrance she had discovered during her wandering the day before.

The sky was clear; a full moon shone brightly, just as it had nearly one month before when they had journeyed to France. Though her stride never faltered, she sucked in a quick breath as though struck by a physical blow. A month! she wanted to wail, a month ago I was with Robert!

Reaching the gazebo that stood on the well-manicured lawn, Caroline entered it and placed her valise under a bench. She retraced her steps quickly and was soon abed.

Chapter Eleven

Garrett Wyndridge looked up as the door to the breakfast parlor opened. Before him Caroline stood unabashedly, her legs clad in doeskin breeches and her coat and cravat tailored to fit a man. Her brown hair curled softly around her face, making her eyes seem larger than ever.

"Is something wrong?" she asked.

Garrett expelled an appreciative whistle then hastened to his feet as she crossed the floor and took a chair.

With his disarming smile, he said, "You must forgive me. I am merely looking at you with new eyes, Caroline. Why are you wearing breeches again, if you don't mind my asking?"

"Not at all, Garrett. My riding habit still hangs on me. Besides, riding astride is much more comfortable."

"So you think you're up to riding? That's good news, indeed. If you'll give me ten minutes, I'll join you," said Garrett.

With utmost calm, Caroline replied, "I don't wish to appear rude to you, Garrett, after all you've done for me, but I really should like to ride alone."

Her open manner gave him no reason to suspect anything, so he acquiesced to her request readily. After a hearty breakfast, Caroline left for the stables.

She smiled, watching the groom lead Morgan toward her.

She mounted the mare, riding astride, and waved farewell to Rosemeade as she rode off.

Caroline took the bridle path into the woods as though she were going to the stock pond. After riding for five minutes, she left the trail and began circling the well-kept grounds, making her way through the woods to the gazebo.

Two gardeners with sickles were working on the east side of the house. Taking a deep breath, she lifted the reins and crossed the green lawn to the summerhouse. One of the men looked up, pulled his forelock respectfully, and returned to his task.

Slipping inside, Caroline retrieved her valise and tied it to the saddle. She maneuvered the little mare close to the structure and, putting one foot on the decorative wrought-iron fence that bordered the flower bed, remounted.

Gathering the reins, she urged the mare back into the woods and was soon away. A half hour later they reached the London road, and Caroline put Morgan along at a brisk trot.

Caroline was very conscious of the fact that she had borrowed, without asking, the viscount's horse. But she could not think of another method of getting away undetected. Livie would never have countenanced her plans, and with Garrett backing Livie, Caroline wasn't certain she could have withstood their combined disapproval.

Her first goal was simply to reach London. To this end, she broke her journey at midmorning at a likely-looking inn at a crossroads.

The innkeeper's robust wife took one look at Caroline's thin face and hurried back to her kitchen. Within minutes, she returned, a young maid following in her wake carrying a heavily laden tray.

"Here we are, sir. I may not cook fancy, but they say my pigeon pie is good enough for the prince hisself. And I thought ye might like some o' my scones with a bit o' my jam."

"Thank you, ma'am. You're very good."

"My pleasure, sir. There's a bit of cheese, too. Now, if you want anything else, you just tell Betsy here."

Thanking her hostess again, Caroline ate what she could manage and settled down to pass an hour. She didn't feel she could trust her equestrian skills with a post-horse, so she had decided to stop every hour or two and rest the game little mare.

Once she had left the inn, Caroline marveled at the ease of traveling by horseback when in the guise of a young gentleman. The payment from the viscount provided the means.

Payment for services rendered.

The phrase echoed in her head like the hoofbeats of the horse. When Garrett had first given her that pouch, she'd wanted to throw it in his face. But her common sense quickly reasserted itself; it was not Garrett, but Robert, in whose face she had wished to throw it. So she had sensibly put it away and planned to dispose of it later. It was not until she began to feel more herself that a new idea had formed.

Caroline had watched Ferdie and Olivia together. The perfect couple, she thought. Olivia loved her husband, but she had interests of her own and didn't depend on Ferdie to entertain her. Ferdie enjoyed having a wife to care for. There didn't appear to be room for a third person. And there shouldn't be, she had reasoned.

But there she was, penniless, or close to it, with a house she could neither afford to keep nor bear to sell. She couldn't live with Olivia.

It had been during these endless ruminations that Caroline's eye had lighted on the bureau with the money and bank draft inside. Unable to justify simply taking it, Caroline decided she must return to White's and finish the work she had begun. Then Garrett had mentioned Robert's return.

The threat had been enough to make her act. She had to get to London and complete her work before he discovered her intentions. Only then could she accept her wages.

By late afternoon, the freedom Caroline was experiencing had worn thin, and she wished for nothing so much as a well-sprung carriage. Her weakened condition was keenly felt.

Just as she began to consider spending the night, she noticed more and more houses along the road, and more traffic as well. Taking heart, she pushed on and was soon crossing Westminster Bridge.

As she drew rein at her cousin's house near Hanover Square, Caroline made no move to dismount. What an incredibly long time I've been gone, she thought wearily. The front door opened, and Biggers, her cousin's starchy butler, peered down the steps curiously. He signaled a footman.

Caroline dismounted, took up the valise herself, and gave the reins to the footman.

"An extra ration of oats for her, please," she called as the footman led the mare around to the stables. "How are you, Biggers?" she asked, feeling lighthearted.

"Very well, sir. And you?"

Biggers was never a big talker, Caroline thought suspiciously. I wonder what he knows. "I'm afraid I had a mishap, but I'm better now."

His next words confirmed her fears. "That's good to know, sir. Mr. Wickersham is in residence, sir."

"Is he? Why, that's good news," she said with a grin, feeling anything but jovial within. "Where is my cousin?"

"In the study, I believe. I'll tell him you're here."

"No need," she said hastily. "I'll announce myself." Saying this, she slipped into the study, hurriedly closing the door on the butler's interested ears.

"Good God! Caroline, is that you?"

She gulped a breath of air, then turned to face her resplendent cousin.

"Yes, Penn, it is I."

"Damn! I thought Biggers had gone stark mad, but it's true! Damn!" He rose to his feet, staring unabashedly.

She managed a nervous smile. "Please, Penn, if you don't mind, could you quit swearing?"

"What? Oh, yes. Sorry, Caroline." He eyed her up and down for a moment, shaking his head. Finally, a tiny gleam appeared in his eyes. It grew into a full-fledged twinkle, and then a smile formed on his lips.

"You know, Caroline, you make a demmed fine boy."

She grinned. "Thank you, Cousin Penn," she said with a bow.

He cleared his throat. "Not that it's to be spread about," he added.

"Of course not, Penn, except for one thing."

He waited; Penn Wickersham never fully trusted his cousin when she got that wide-eyed innocent look. She was just a bit too clever for his liking.

"Everyone already believes that your cousin is a boy, a young man, to be exact. Only the name is Charles Pennington."

"Everyone?"

"Yes, everyone at White's, that is. That's where I was working, in the library there, during the time Miss Stanton and I were in London."

"At White's?" he reiterated weakly.

"Yes, I was cataloguing the library. Viscount Rosemeade employed me to do so. I've come back to finish the job."

"Viscount . . ." said Penn.

"Rosemeade," said Caroline.

Penn Wickersham considered himself a Corinthian, up to any rig or row and unconcerned with the opinions of society. But here was his cousin, brought up as a lady, telling him she had not only entered those hallowed portals of White's but had actually been employed there. And she had been hired by Viscount Rosemeade. While Rosemeade was not a Corinthian, he was respected by everyone, a gentleman who stayed within the lines of propriety without being prudish or stiff-necked. And he had hired Caroline?

"Say something, Penn. Don't just stare."

"Sorry, Caroline, but you must admit your story is remarkable."

She smiled appreciatively. "How delicate you are!"

"No, no, I'm not. Damn, Caroline! What were you thinking?"

She clenched her teeth, sudden anger springing forth that her cousin should question her motives. "I was trying to keep Papa's house and earn enough to start a small school. I'm sorry if I've shocked or embarrassed you; I'll be going."

She turned on her heel and headed for the door, her pride warding off a growing desperation. But Penn Wickersham was, deep down, a gentleman, and he was truly fond of his cousin. He reached the door before her.

"Wait, Caroline, don't go! I meant no affront; I'm just trying to understand."

His kindness was harder for her to take than his incredulous questions. Her eyes filled with tears, and she struggled against blinking, for that would send the tears streaming down her cheeks.

Penn was unused to females, especially weeping ones, and he stood helpless, hands hanging limply at his side.

"Caroline, you should have come to me. I would have helped," he said.

Unable to speak, she merely shook her head. Finally, she managed a rueful smile. "With you still on an allowance from your grandfather? If it weren't for your mother, you wouldn't even have this house."

"True, but dash it all, I would have managed something. Our mothers were sisters, after all."

"Yes, Penn, and that's why I've turned to you now. I've got to finish the commission I started."

"Then the viscount hasn't paid you yet?"

"Not in full," she lied, disliking the necessity for prevarication again but feeling unequal to risk losing her cousin's cooperation.

"No doubt the balance will be paid on completion of the work," said Penn.

"Yes, so you see, I need to stay in London till the job is finished, and I was hoping to stay here," she said in a rush.

"Here? Good God, Caroline! You can't be serious. Why, your reputation—and mine—would be in shreds! A female staying here!"

Careful, Caroline told herself, don't press too hard. She struck a thoughtful pose.

"Hmm. I hadn't thought of that. I suppose I've been dressed in breeches so long, I've begun to see myself as others must."

Satisfied he had forestalled his cousin's horrid plan, Penn nodded eagerly. With her here, he would have had to change his life-style drastically. No more card games, no friends drinking all night and sleeping it off wherever they might fall.

"I'm glad you see it my way, Caroline. Now, if there's anything else I can do, I'd—"

"There's one thing," she interrupted. "Could you recommend a good, clean hotel? Nothing fancy, a posting house, perhaps."

"A . . . a posting house?"

"Yes, I must admit I hate stabling the viscount's mare at such a place, but it can't be helped," she added briskly.

"The viscount's mare?"

"Yes, yes, Penn, I do wish you wouldn't echo everything I say. It's an extremely annoying habit."

"I'm not . . . Oh, never mind. Caroline, you can't stay at a posting house."

"Nonsense! I'm sure there's at least one in London that I'll find acceptable."

"No, Caroline, I can't allow it. You'll stay here," he announced firmly.

"But you said—"

"Never mind what I said. You'll stay here. I'd go to a hotel, but I'm rather short this quarter. Besides, I couldn't leave you here alone without a chaperone."

"You're so sweet, Penn."

"Hmph! You can drop those damsel-in-distress airs with me, Caroline Pennington. I know you too well!"

Ignoring his gruff exterior, she threw her arms around his neck and gave him a quick hug. A blush spread across his face as he plucked her arms from around his neck.

"Here now, stop that! What would Biggers think if he came in?"

"With fusty-faced Biggers, who knows?" she retorted gaily.

"Come on now. You must be done in. Did you really ride horseback to London?" he asked incredulously. As she began to answer, he stopped her. "No, don't tell me now. Save it for later, at dinner."

"Now, Penn, if you've got plans, don't feel you have to play host to me."

"There's nothing I'd rather do than have dinner with my best cousin, Mr. Pennington."

He opened the study door and told a footman to take Caroline's valise up. Caroline followed the servant up the stairs, her step weary now that the crucial encounter with Penn was over.

Biggers stood in the entrance hall, his face a careful study of indifference.

Turning to the butler, Penn said, "Biggers, come into the study and shut the door."

When they were alone, Penn spoke again, his voice commanding.

"My cousin will be staying here for the next two or three weeks. I believe you've guessed Mr. Pennington is a female, but she is a lady, Biggers, and I want her treated accordingly, even though she's wearing, ahem, men's clothes."

"Will that be all, sir?" said the regal butler.

"No, I'm afraid not. I'm counting on you to keep the other servants in line. And me, too, for that matter. We shall have regular hours for meals, of course, and I'll not be having any of my friends over. But, Biggers, you know how I am when I'm a trifle bosky; if I should show up one night with, shall we say, unexpected company, I count on you to steer me or them away."

"My pleasure, sir."

Feeling he had somehow failed to win over his servant's wholehearted support (and who could tell with Biggers?), Penn said defensively, "She's a damned nice girl, Biggers, and proud."

Giving what might have passed for a smile, Biggers said, "So I thought the first time I met her." He bowed, leaving his employer gaping in astonishment.

Caroline felt carefree as she made her way to the club the next morning. She had always enjoyed Penn's company, and he had been especially amusing the night before.

He had demanded to know why she had been gone so long at Rosemeade, but Caroline was prepared for this query. Telling him she had fallen ill, she refrained from mentioning the jaunt to the coast of France or the subsequent bullet wound. Instinctively, she realized that, as her relative, a male relative, he would not understand her traveling alone with Robert. She also explained Miss Stanton's absence, saying she had married and was on an extended honeymoon.

If there was anything in her narrative that Penn found difficult to swallow, he kept silent about it. Instead, he had described to her the latest *on-dit,* most of which was about an outrageous wager among his friends.

Caroline hesitated as she reached the top step of the club, but the doorman was already opening the door. He greeted her respectfully, and she breathed a sigh of relief.

On the way to the library, she encountered the faithful Boggs. His scraggly brows shot up when he caught sight of her.

"Mr. Pennington, lad, I thought ye'd finished 'ere, ye've been away so long."

"No, not finished yet. Though it won't take much longer." Feeling something else was owed the kind old servant, she explained, "I fell ill, and it's taken me a while to get back on my feet. Now, how about a cup of hot tea before I get back to work."

"Aye, sir. In a twinklin'."

As he hurried off, Caroline smiled. She was certain that he, too, had guessed her secret, possibly before she had gone to Rosemeade. But his knowledge didn't trouble her in the least. Boggs would never betray her; on the contrary, she was confident he would do all he could to shield her.

Once inside the library where she had spent so many hours, Caroline sat down on the couch, lost in bittersweet reminiscences.

In every corner, she could visualize the viscount. Odd, she thought, I've no recollection of the comte in here, though he often materialized to spoil my day. But Robert? She smiled secretly and hugged her knees up against her chest.

She recalled his distress when he realized she was outraged by his insulting her in front of the comte. Then she looked toward the door and visualized him as he had entered that day it had rained so. His gray eyes had been blazing with anger, and her coolness had only infuriated him more. Finally, he had seen how ridiculous he was being and had burst out laughing, his deep, throaty laugh that could always send her spirits soaring.

The thought of his laughter—and the eternal absence of it—plunged her into the depths of despair. There was a quiet knock and Boggs entered, carrying the tea tray. Caroline jumped up and began a close inspection of one shelf.

"I brought some of those macaroons ye liked so much, sir. Did ye want me to pour?"

"No, thank you," she managed to say.

Shaking his head, the old man shuffled out the door. He didn't know what the viscount had done, but he wished fervently that he might have a word with his lordship at that moment. Making that young girl cry!

In the week that followed, Caroline slipped into a comfortable routine. She finished shelving all the books, periodicals, and journals, then began recording each title, author, and volume number on small cards, which she kept in a wooden box.

One section of shelving was for novels; since White's was a men's club, this was rather empty. But she was able to place there two copies of Sir Walter Scott's *Marmion*, the dog-eared copy of *Tristram Shandy*, and one volume of Miss Austen's *Sense and Sensibility*. There were two copies of Voltaire's *Candide* (one in French and one English translation) and even a copy of Richardson's *Pamela, or Virtue Rewarded*.

Political treatises such as Thomas Paine's *Common Sense* and *The Age of Reason* and John Locke's *Treatises of Government* filled a large section. Almost an entire wall was taken up with Greek and Latin classics, most of which, Caroline surmised, were castoffs from days spent at Cambridge or Oxford. Alphabetizing these had been a horror; the authorship of so many was questionable. Finally, she decided to divide them by topics, and thence by titles. There was poetry by Virgil and Horace and tragedies by Aeschylus, Sophocles, and Euripides. She also made a space for satires and comedies such as *Amphitruo* by Plautus and *Thesmophoriazusae* by Aristophanes. Philosophical and historical classics had to be dealt with as well, and Caroline carefully marked each volume and made a card for it to place in her file.

She saw almost no one, and it was several days before she discovered Boggs was carefully screening visitors. She confronted him about it.

"Boggs, I appreciate your efforts, but you mustn't spend all day hovering about outside my door."

"I don't tell 'em they can't go in, miss"—he had given up all pretense of calling her sir—"them that has real business in there get inside."

She shook her head, resigned to the hopelessness of convincing him.

"Very well, Boggs. Just don't get anyone angry at my being in here all the time. Another week and I should finish. Then we can both relax."

"Amen to that, miss!" came the heartfelt reply.

The next morning, she placed the last few Latin and Greek works in their proper slots and felt a surge of relief. She had taken home a Greek treatise on horsemanship by Xenophon and waded through it the night before. It was an interesting mental exercise, but she greatly preferred reading the Duke of Newcastle's *New Method—A General System of Horsemanship in All Its Branches*. This work was informative though not as exciting as learning the finer points from the viscount.

As Caroline finished the card and replaced Homer's *The Odyssey*, she grimaced with distaste. Papa had told her she would never be a true scholar of the classics if she didn't appreciate Homer's recounting of Odysseus's wanderings. She had replied with a sassy face and said, "Then you must resign yourself to the fact, Papa. I shall always find Homer monotonous and trite."

At the thought of her father, the reason for her reflective mood surfaced. Today is August 13, she realized suddenly. It had been exactly one year ago that Dr. Hammond had brought her the awful news. Papa had died one year ago, to the day.

"Oh, Papa," she whispered to the air. "If only you were alive, I wouldn't be in this miserable predicament. I would never have met Viscount Rosemeade, would never have fallen in love."

Afraid she would be discovered crying, Caroline deliberately put away the card box and made her way out of the club and onto the street.

The morning air was refreshing, and she managed to stave off the tears. But her spirits were low, and she began to walk briskly down the street, not caring which direction she chanced to take.

Fatigue finally slowed her pace, and Caroline

took stock of her whereabouts. Startled, she gazed up at the elegant façade of the viscount's town house off Grosvenor Square. She could not have recounted how she had arrived there, but her first instinct was to get away.

"Caroline!"

Too late, she thought. She pivoted and found herself looking into the eyes of Ferdie Farningham.

"Hello, Ferdie," she said with a bland smile, retreating a step.

"Wait a minute, young lady," he insisted. Two passersby appeared intrigued by his odd manner of addressing another man. After shooting them a speaking look, he began to drag her toward the house.

"Ferdie, I'm not going in there!" she said through clenched teeth.

"Oh, yes, you are!" he retorted with grim determination.

Though Caroline was two or three inches taller, Ferdie was quite strong. She soon gave in and marched up the steps with dignity. The double doors opened immediately, and Lane, his lordship's butler, greeted them.

"Lane, Mr. Pennington and I will be in the library. Bring us some brandy."

"Very good, Mr. Farningham," replied the stately servant, never batting an eye.

Caroline followed silently, bracing herself for her encounter with the viscount. She fought down a last-minute desire to run as Ferdie threw open the door. In the next second, she realized the room was quite empty. Torn between relief and disappointment, she dropped into the nearest chair, all bravado vanished.

"That was a selfish thing to do, Caroline," Ferdie began. "Olivia has been frantic since Captain Wyndridge notified us that you'd vanished, and he's chasing all over the countryside for his brother."

"Robert?" she said coldly. "Robert has nothing to do with this."

Ferdie shook his head in disbelief.

"We both know better, but that's not what I meant. My concern is with Olivia. She hoped you had returned to your father's house, so she is in Cambridge. Garrett has gone to Northumberland, hoping to find Robert. I was to inquire around London, discreetly, of course. Livie wanted me to call in Bow Street, but it's rather awkward. Who do I tell them to find, Mr. or Miss Pennington?"

Caroline smiled to hear Ferdie rattling on so. He was truly agitated.

"Well, you needn't worry now, Ferdie. You have found me. I am fine. And I really should be going. Oh, there is one thing. I borrowed Robert's horse. If you would tell the stablehands here, I'll drop her by in the morning."

"You know I will, but, Caroline, you still haven't told me why you're here in London."

She rose, but he was before her at the door. He would find out soon enough.

"Finishing what I started," she replied simply.

"Why couldn't you tell us in that note?"

"Ferdie, I'm sorry I've caused so much trouble. If I had told Garrett my plans, he would have moved heaven and earth to stop me. And I have to finish."

She had won his sympathy.

Ferdie placed his hand lightly on her arm. "How much longer will you be at it?"

Her eyes glistened with unshed tears, and she smiled at him gratefully. "Another week should do it. I'm fine, Ferdie. I'm staying with my cousin Penn."

Anyone else would have protested such a scandalous arrangement, but Ferdie was already too distracted, and knowing Penn Wickersham to be an honest sportsman, there could be nothing wrong with Caroline's lodging with him. He merely nodded and opened the library door, allowing her to pass.

As she made her way to the huge front door, he called, "Write to Olivia. She's been worried."

Caroline promised to do so and escaped.

In the next few days, Caroline's progress was hampered by constant interruptions from her well-meaning friends. Finally, she rebelled, demanding that Ferdie and Cousin Penn be banned from the library at White's.

As usual, Boggs carried out her request, and her work swiftly drew to a close.

Dusk was settling over the city as Caroline returned to her cousin's house that last evening. Her task was finished; a final check the next day, and she could be on her way. No more Charles Pennington.

Caroline refused to admit she would miss her masquerade. Resolutely, she sampled one of Cook's macaroons as she perused the *Post*. She read with interest an article purported to be an eyewitness account of Wellesley's capture of Madrid on August 12. The clock struck ten; she yawned, resting her cheek on her hand. Her eyes fell upon the social column, and she sat upright in her chair.

"Lord R. returned to the city today. Good fishing, Lady L."

Lord R.! It had to be Robert! And the other sly reference? Augusta, of course!

So Robert had returned. It was the one thing Caroline dreaded. Each time the door to the library at White's opened, she had looked up sharply, half expecting to see his face. And now . . .

Unable to sit still, she rose and took herself downstairs to the cozy salon where she and Olivia had shared many evenings. She spied a deck of cards on a table and picked them up. Without thinking, she began to shuffle them and laid out a game of patience.

Red queen on black king . . .

Perhaps he won't find out, she thought.

Black seven on red eight . . . Of course he will! she told herself sternly. Don't be ridiculous!

Turn the cards, three at a time . . .

But surely he won't care if I'm here.

Straighten the rows; king in the open column . . .

Oh, not much! He'll drag me out by my hair!

As this humiliating image flashed before her eyes, Caroline pitched the cards onto the table and began to prowl about the room.

Really! It was so vexatious to be in love. She had grown up among stodgy old professors (and Robert's recent behavior reminded her of a certain Professor Dodd), but she could even handle them. But here she was, pacing back and forth like one of the wild animals at the Exchange, unable even to concentrate on cards. It was worse than when the comte was blackmailing her.

Love in the novels she'd read was never like this! How had she gotten herself into such a fix?

Caroline forced herself to sit down and heaved a sigh. "Lord R." was very likely in the arms of "Lady L." at that moment, while she sat playing at cards. Why couldn't love play fair? Since she couldn't have Robert, why must she love him so? For despite everything, Caroline admitted, she still loved him; she always would.

Caroline glanced at the clock.

Robert has no doubt seen Ferdie by now, she thought. Involuntarily, Caroline peered at the closed door of the salon, fully expecting to see it thrust open and Robert appear, angry and irrational. She had gone against his orders and returned to White's. He would be livid. His beautiful gray eyes, capable of lighting with kindness, would stare straight through her.

Caroline shuddered.

Chapter Twelve

Indeed, Caroline would have quaked at that moment if it had been she having an audience with the viscount. But it was Ferdie, stolid, well meaning, and surprisingly unimpressed by his friend's rage.

"Robert," said Ferdie as the viscount paused to catch his breath, "I've never known you to be so hot-blooded. You're always the one who's unrattled. Now look at you."

Rosemeade glared down at his friend; his manner grew calm but icy.

"Ferdie, you can keep your damned opinions to yourself. I'm late for an appointment."

"And Caroline?" persisted Ferdie.

"I shall save the pleasure of paying a call on Miss Pennington until tomorrow morning."

With this, the viscount stormed out, leaving Ferdie to fret the night away.

Shortly after midnight, the door to the viscount's library opened. Ferdie looked up quickly, ready to try out new arguments on his obstinate friend.

"Ferdie! What the devil are you doing here?"

"Garrett, where did you come from?"

Captain Wyndridge stalked into the room, a scowl marring his handsome features. He didn't speak until he had flopped into an easy chair and stretched his long legs out on the ottoman.

"Where? You name it, and I've been there! After Cambridge, I went to Randolph's place in Scotland. No Robert! I followed him to Leicestershire, but they said he'd gone home to Rosemeade. So I went back there. But he'd left Rosemeade this morning. I've been all over this bloody countryside, and I promise you, Ferdie, if you tell me Robert isn't here, I'll plant you a facer."

"He's not here—"

"Damn!"

"Right now, that is. I believe he's with Augusta."

Garrett breathed a sigh of relief. Lane entered, followed by a footman carrying a heavy tray.

"Wonderful, Lane! Tell Cook she's a dear. I'm starved," said Garrett.

"Indeed, sir. I shall convey the sentiment."

Ferdie, too, was on his feet eyeing the tray of thin-sliced meats, cheeses, and fruits appreciatively.

"That's all, Lane. Thank you."

The two gentlemen began to eat; neither spoke for several minutes. Then, his immediate fear of expiring from malnutrition gone, Garrett grinned at Ferdie.

"Why are you so hungry? I'm the one who rode all the way from Rosemeade."

"Ha! Perhaps, but I could hardly eat supper tonight after facing Robert this evening. He was on a tear when I told him about Miss Pennington."

"Miss Pennington?"

"I've found her, too. She insists on completing her work at White's, you see. That made him mad, too. Matter of fact, everything I said made him mad," said Ferdie.

"Hmm. Mad, was he? I thought he would be worried, to be sure, but why is he angry?"

Ferdie shook his head, waving a stubby finger at the captain.

"With Robert, who knows. Miss Pennington is staying with her cousin, Penn Wickersham."

"Penn . . . Is he married now?" asked Garrett.

"No, and that didn't soothe my lord's temper one bit. You know he told her to forget about that damned library. But the chit's got some maggot that she can't accept that money unless she finishes the job."

A glimmer of a smile played on Garrett's lips.

"And that makes my brother furious, I'll be bound."

"Let us say he was moved to express himself in emphatic terms," said Ferdie dryly.

"You know, Ferdie, Olivia and I were right. Now, if we can just keep those two from killing one another, this ridiculous little melodrama might turn out quite well."

"I wish you more luck than I had," said Ferdie.

"Thanks. Now, first thing in the morning . . ."

"Rivers, did my brother show up last night?" the viscount asked as he shrugged into his coat the next morning.

"I believe so, my lord," said his valet.

The Scandalous Miss

"I thought I recognized that horse. And Mr. Farningham, did he stay the night?"

"No, my lord. I believe he went home."

"Good," said the viscount as he began to tie his cravat. The valet retreated as this important ritual was performed.

"Blast! Get me a fresh one, Rivers." As the valet scurried to obey, the clock at the top of the staircase struck nine.

"Go and see if my brother is up and about yet."

Rivers returned as Rosemeade gave a satisfied grunt at his reflection in the mirror.

"He's still abed, my lord. Do you wish me to wake him?"

"Lord, no! I've no wish to listen to him or Ferdie! I just wanted to make sure I can walk out my own door without being waylaid."

"I see, my lord," said Rivers, not truly understanding any of it.

"Rivers, one thing. Send someone to Gauthier's. I want two dozen yellow roses delivered to Lady Lietchfield."

"Very good, my lord. And an enclosure?"

Robert paused, his hand on the door, then retraced his steps and sat down in front of a small escritoire. Swiftly he penned:

You were right. Thanks.

Robert

He handed the card to Rivers, who read it with a puzzled look.

Rosemeade whistled softly as he sailed along the corridor; it grew in volume as he bounded down the stairs, taking them two at a time.

Caroline had slept badly. She had dreamed of a terrible argument with the viscount.

Dawn was breaking when she started awake from this black dream. Caroline scurried to the fireplace and poked at the dying embers until a tiny blaze appeared. Adding a small log, she huddled before the meager fire, wrapped in misery.

At seven, she got up and dressed with care. This would be the day she finished the library.

A proud accomplishment, Caroline informed her image in the mirror. Her snowy cravat was tied perfectly; her dark brown hair secured by a black grosgrain ribbon. She nodded to her reflection and squared her shoulders, thinking how well her brown superfine coat looked.

With head held high, she marched down the stairs to the front door. She glanced at her papa's pocket watch: eight o'clock. It was early, but not too early to get to work.

The dining room, lounge, and game room were deserted. Caroline tried to store up each image. Who knows, she thought, I might write a book about all this someday.

The library was dark; businesslike, she strode to the windows and threw back the shutters, letting the early-morning light flood the room.

Satisfied, she turned to the shelves, carefully checking the spine of each volume, making certain it held the correct identification number. As she worked, she corrected two or three, and time passed quickly.

The last shelf! she realized with a start. Suddenly, she was finished. She flipped through the file of cards; everything was in order there, too.

A quiet knock heralded the entrance of Boggs.

"You're at it early, miss. I didn't see ye come in."

She smiled at him over her shoulder.

"I'm finished, Boggs," she announced quietly.

"It looks right nice, miss." A bit flustered by Caroline's sobriety, he said gruffly, "How about a pot o' tea and some o' Cook's macaroons that ye like so much?"

With her back to Boggs, Caroline smiled sadly at the shelves. She sighed, then shrugged her shoulders, shaking off her gloom.

"The macaroons will be fine. I've not broken my fast yet this morning. But tea?" She turned to face him, a saucy grin breaking forth. "Make it champagne, Boggs. I should celebrate!"

"Right ye are, miss!" he replied, his scraggly brows shooting up as his eyes rounded with approval.

In the servant's absence, Caroline pulled out her watch. Only ten o'clock. I can probably catch a stage to Cambridge this afternoon, she thought. Hands on her hips, she stood back from the shelves and proudly surveyed her handiwork.

"A little early, isn't it, Boggs?"

Boggs jumped, then looked up warily into the viscount's cool gray eyes.

"M'lord," he said casually, he hoped, all the while maneuvering himself to block the viscount's passage to the library.

"Champagne? Are we celebrating something?"

Bristling at this sarcasm, Boggs threw out his chest defiantly. "Aye, m'lord, that we are. And I'd be best pleased if ye'd just turn about and leave her be."

"I think not, Boggs. As a matter of fact, I believe I'll just relieve you of your burden. You don't mind, I trust," he said, wresting the tray from the reluctant servant.

Boggs hovered uncertainly by the door.

"M'lord, if ye do anything . . ." He let the empty threat hang and moved back, lowering his head.

"Rest easy, old friend," said the viscount.

Boggs looked up sharply, unable to read his lordship's hooded expression. Then he opened the door, allowing the viscount to pass through before pulling it closed again.

Caroline continued to gaze at the shelves though her thoughts were miles away. She listened only vaguely as the champagne bubbled its way into the glass.

A hand came from behind, offering her a glass. She reached out to take the crystal goblet; then, glancing at the hand, she saw the heavy gold signet ring. Her grip faltered and the glass fell, shattering on the floor.

Caroline whirled around.

"Robert," she breathed, her brown eyes riveted on his face.

The crunch of glass under her foot made her look down. Nervously, she stooped and began to collect the broken glass.

"Caroline," said the viscount, his deep voice compelling her to look up.

As she did, a piece of glass found its way into her thumb.

"Ouch!" she yelped, dropping all the pieces as she watched the blood seep out.

The viscount pulled out his handkerchief and knelt down as she produced her own handkerchief. Shoving the cloth back into his pocket, he watched as she pressed the material against the small cut.

Awkwardly, they stood up. The viscount looked at the neat shelves lining the walls.

"I see you've finished," he said needlessly.

"Yes, my lord," answered Caroline, her voice a little too high. "I promised to fulfill the commission, and I have."

"And now? Your school?"

"No, not this year. Not without Livie," she said.

Rosemeade nodded. Changing the topic, he commented, "Boggs knows, I see."

"Yes, actually a half-dozen or so do, but you needn't worry. They wouldn't betray me. And I'll be leaving this evening on the stage. As a matter of fact, my lord, I must go and pack."

Manfully, Caroline extended her hand. When the viscount failed to respond, she withdrew it slowly. Without another word, she walked toward the door.

"Caroline."

She stopped. It had been so soft. . . . Had he really spoken?

"Caroline, come here." There was no denying that deep, quiet tone. Unwilling to hope, she merely looked over her shoulder into those smoky-gray eyes.

"Please," he added.

Without a word she returned to stand before him. He placed one hand under her chin. With the other, he reached around to the nape of her neck and untied the restrictive ribbon.

Caroline watched his face, his lips, draw closer. She closed her eyes, savoring the exquisite anticipation.

His lips met hers, a touch so feather-soft her eyes flew open, questioning and concerned. His gaze was warm, intrigued.

"That's what I should have done the night we quarreled," he said.

Understanding dawned. Filled with sudden assurance, Caroline laced her fingers behind his neck and pulled him down to meet her waiting lips.

Tentative at first, then with growing desire, she let her kiss communicate all her hopes and her passion. Not to be outdone, he swept her into his arms and returned her kisses with a fervor to match her own.

Caroline was startled to feel Robert's tongue probe between her parted lips. Unsure at first if she liked this invasion, she responded in kind, her efforts experimental. Then she drew back, leaving him to kiss her cheek, her ear, her neck.

"Robert," she whispered between gasps for air, "Robert, please, will you marry me?"

He stopped in midkiss, looking at her quizzically.

His voice quivering with amusement, he replied solemnly, "Yes, Caroline, I'll marry you."

As she dived for another kiss, he took hold of her chin and gazed into her eyes.

"But from now on, I carry the handkerchiefs, I do the proposing, and, last but not least, I wear the breeches!"

Caroline's eyes twinkled, but she promised, "Yes, my lord."

"And no more 'my lords,' young lady!"

In response to her giggle, he began kissing her fiercely.